Waiting in the Shadows

Sarah Lamb

A thank you to my proofreader, Brooke, and all of the lovely women who help ARC read to catch those typos I miss!

This book was not written by AI. Any typos are proudly (and embarrassingly!) my own human created ones!

This book is not allowed to be used in training AI.

Paperback ISBN: 978-1-960418-61-6

Large print ISBN: 978-1-960418-62-3

Contents

For those who have a secret hope.
May it soon come true.

Chapter 1

1870s Deepwater, Missouri

Ellen Grayson held as still as she could. The rattlesnake slid closer, its long form curving and its tail shaking in a terrifying yet mesmerizing way. Its tongue darted out, and the mouth opened as a hiss filled her ears. Ellen's eyes stayed on the fangs about to pierce her.

She'd never been so scared in all the twenty-two years of her life. Would she be able to find her way home in time to get help if it struck her?

It was unlikely. The venom would work too quickly. What would her parents say? Do? Would they miss her? Worry? Blame the Claytons? They blamed everything on the Claytons, even the weather. It was likely this would be no different.

The snake's head jerked back, its jaws opened wide, and she wanted to close her eyes, but Ellen decided to meet her fate head on. Maybe, by some miracle, she could even dodge the attack.

The snake coiled, and it was all she could do not to scream. It rose and—

TWACK!

With a start, Ellen gaped at the hatchet that had cleaved the snake in two, the blade buried in the forest's ground and the handle still vibrating slightly. Then, feeling perhaps even more fear than she had at the snake, she pulled her eyes up, and stared into two dark eyes as Derek Clayton stepped closer.

He was tall and muscular, with eyes and hair the color of coal. She'd always marveled at that, as no one else in town had hair that color. All the Claytons were the same. Suited them, her pa said. Their hearts were black as well.

Her pulse pounded loudly in her ears. Was he going to use the hatchet on her next? That's what his kind did, wasn't it? Her parents would say so. His family was filled with the worst kinds of people, her ma said. Did that include murderers?

Derek glanced at the snake, and toed it, kicking one half away from the other as though checking to be sure it was dead.

"You hurt?" he asked, his eyes darting over her trembling body.

Ellen shook her head no. She wasn't, yet. Her mouth felt dry, and her tongue frozen. Should she let loose a scream? Could she even? When Derek didn't say anything, she relaxed slightly. Maybe he wasn't going to hurt her.

"Why...why'd you save me?" she asked, finally summoning the words to her mouth. "You're a Clayton."

He swallowed visibly, then shrugged. "You haven't ever done me wrong." Then he glanced around. "You alone? What are you doing here? This is Clayton land."

"I'm lost," Ellen said. She tried to keep her voice from wobbling. "I was getting Ma some berries, and somehow I got twisted around. Then I ended up here."

He nodded, and pointed behind her. "Turn around and go straight. Don't veer at all. You'll get to a big tree in the shape of a Y. Go left. Keep going, and you'll find that berry patch at the border of our land and town."

"Thank you," Ellen said, and picked up her small bucket. "You saved my life. I owe you."

For a second, he flashed a grin before his eyes narrowed slightly. "That right?"

She nodded, and boldly stepped toward him so he wouldn't think she was afraid. It wouldn't do. "That's right."

"Give me a kiss then," he said. "Bet you won't."

Ellen's heart started thudding again, but this time for an entirely different reason. Derek Clayton was the most handsome boy around.

For years, she'd had trouble not staring each time she sat behind him at church. It wasn't just his good looks that caught her eye. Honestly, she wasn't quite sure what it was. But he'd never talked to her much until today.

Courage surged through her. "Bet you I will," she answered, stepping closer. Before she could rethink her decision, Ellen rose on her toes and kissed his cheek dangerously close to the side of his lips, then stepped back. A long strand of her auburn hair caught the breeze, and danced along her face.

Derek's cheeks were red, and she suspected hers were as well. But Ellen didn't care. That had been her first time giving anyone other than her parents a kiss, and it was something she'd remember forever. Soft, warm, and over far too soon.

"You did it," he said, surprise in his voice.

She repeated his words from earlier, with a small toss of her head. "You haven't ever done me wrong. In fact, you saved my life."

There was a sound behind him, dry leaves and the snapping of old wood from a short distance. He glanced over his shoulder, then back at her with urgency in his voice and expression. "To the tree with the Y, turn left. Hurry now."

Ellen didn't hesitate. If there was another Clayton, Derek wouldn't be able to let her go, and she didn't want him to change his mind. She also didn't want him to get in trouble, for having let her leave unhindered. Skirts in one hand, berry bucket in the other, she flew in the direction he told her.

About a dozen paces away, she quickly peeked over her shoulder and saw him still watching her. A moment later, he was gone. Had it been a dream? If it weren't for her burning lips, Ellen might have thought so.

A Clayton had saved her life. Ellen could hardly believe it. No one would believe a Clayton had saved a Grayson. Not a single soul. But she also knew she couldn't ever tell anyone. If her pa found out, especially that she'd kissed him, he'd try and hurt Derek. With how much her family hated his, he'd likely succeed too.

Ellen couldn't have that. Not when she thought she could like Derek. Maybe had from the moment she'd first set eyes on him. If only she wasn't forbidden from seeing him again.

The berry bushes loomed before her, as did the very clearly marked boundary between the town and the Clayton land. Ellen hurried to the neutral area, the town's land, and grabbed berries by the handful, throwing them into the bucket in her haste, and hoping they wouldn't bruise. If anyone came, it would look like she'd been there for a time. Not on forbidden land.

It didn't take long for the small pail to fill, and Ellen's eyes searched the forest beyond, straining to see if Derek was there still. She hoped to see him again.

Even more importantly, she hoped to kiss him again. That would never happen, she knew it, but she could think about it just the same. Ellen didn't quite know what had happened back there, but she knew the moment had changed everything. Not only had she fallen deeper for Derek, after he'd saved her life, but now she was wondering. Had to know.

Why were their families enemies? If it were something that could be fixed...then there'd be no reason she couldn't spend more time with him. Perhaps have more of those kisses that burned in her, longing to be deposited on him.

But that was likely wishful thinking. As much as Ellen ached for it to be different, for generations, their families had a feud, and something like today wasn't likely enough to change that. No matter how much she hoped it would.

Chapter 2

The sound of footsteps moved closer, and Derek quickly picked up the hatchet and cut the tail off the rattler. A few seconds later, Hugh, his older brother, appeared. "Thought I heard talking," Hugh said, looking around.

"That was me. Killed a rattler," Derek said, holding up the tail.

"See a nest?" his brother asked, glancing around.

"Didn't." Derek's eyes flicked in the direction he'd last seen Ellen. He hoped she'd found her way back to the berry patch. When he'd come across her, frozen to the spot and terrified, he hadn't thought twice. He'd flung his hatchet, and all those years of practicing his aim paid off. It had cleaved the vermin in two. He'd been glad he hadn't missed, and that the snake hadn't struck Ellen. He wouldn't have been able to get her back to town and get help before it was too late for her.

And he couldn't have been seen with Ellen, either. Didn't matter that he'd have been trying to save her life. That might have been worse, and her folks thinking he'd tried to end it.

Derek was sure he'd never forget her terrified face. And he knew the all too brief moment of her lips on his skin would haunt him for the rest of his days. Derek didn't know why he'd said what he had about her kissing him, but maybe it was because over the years his eyes had always sought her out, and Derek had wondered—more than once—just what it would have been like to talk to her, touch her, kiss her. All the things he longed to do.

But she was a Grayson and he was a Clayton. Their kind were oil and water. Couldn't mix. Even thinking about it only had the potential to make things worse.

"Saw bobcat tracks," Hugh said, starting back toward their house, but pointing over to the east. "Best not go anywhere without a rifle."

A rifle. That would make it even more dangerous for Ellen, or anyone else who found themselves on their land, because Derek knew neither his brother nor his father would hesitate to shoot anything or anyone on their land. Even if they were unarmed.

"Thanks for the warning," Derek said, following his brother.

They walked in silence, though Derek couldn't stop wondering if his brother had seen a glimpse of Ellen as she'd dashed away, in that pretty pink dress of hers he loved so much. There were thin lines that ran up and down, in pinks and white that made her look even taller than she was. Which appeared to be just the perfect size. It had sure felt it when she was next to him.

"What are you thinking?" Hugh asked. "You're quiet."

Derek caught himself as he started to startle. "Just hungry," he answered.

He couldn't tell his brother what he was thinking. They might be close, but Hugh couldn't be trusted with this secret. It might slip past his lips, and his parents wouldn't be happy if they knew what he'd done. Didn't matter to them that a life might have been at stake, if it was a Grayson.

"Me too," Hugh agreed as they neared their front porch. "Hope Ma has lunch ready."

Derek nodded, and a couple minutes later was sitting at the kitchen table with a plate heaped with gravy noodles in front of him.

As he dug in, Hugh said, "Pa, might need some traps in the woods."

Derek's fork stilled. Traps? That would also be a bad idea. If Ellen had gotten caught in a trap, she might have lost her foot.

"Why?" his father asked. "What'd you see?"

"Just some vermin," Derek answered. "Not sure we need traps."

"Vermin? Was it the Graysons?" his father asked, hooting in laughter

"Bobcat tracks," Hugh said, "and Derek got a rattler."

"Traps might not be a bad idea," his father agreed, his face now serious. "Take care of that and more." His eyes seemed to glint.

"Yeah, but what if someone gets lost and trapped in one?" Derek said. "You remember a while back, when the tailor's little girl got lost and the woods got searched?"

"Wouldn't it be fine if a Grayson wandered over here and stepped in one?" his father said, not seeming to hear him.

Derek's mother gasped. "Joe, maybe we shouldn't! What if it was someone from town?" she asked. "Wouldn't do to capture a child! Heaven help us if the reverend got caught in a trap!"

His father rubbed at his jaw and nodded. "Reckon you're right. Can't all of them kids read the no trespassing signs yet. Ain't been that long that Deepwater had a teacher. But I'm still going to smile about the idea of catching a Grayson." He laughed again.

Hoping his relief wouldn't show, Derek hunched over his meal. It was no exaggeration that he enjoyed his mother's cooking, so shoveling it in wasn't anything unusual. He half listened as Hugh talked about the bobcat tracks, and keeping a closer eye on their chickens, while the other half of him drifted back to Ellen's teasing tone, her sweet face, though her cheeks were tinged with pink, and the feel of her so close.

"...and the Ellen's."

Derek's head shot up. "What?" His heart started hammering. Hugh had seen! Why did he wait until now to say her name?

"Was saying their horse died, and now they can't plow." Hugh shook his head. "Also, the Elkins are about out of food, Reverend Sullivan said, since Mr. Elkins hasn't been able to work for a few months because of his injury. Mrs. Sullivan is hoping to help fill a few baskets with grub to give them Sunday."

Elkins. Not Ellen's. Derek wanted to relax, but didn't feel he could. The stress was too much. He wasn't sure how he could keep this secret. But he had to. Ellen's life might depend on it.

"I'll bake extra bread tonight," his mother said. "Joe, how much is in the smokehouse?"

"Enough to share," his father said. He stood then. "I'm going back to the field. I'll get something from there in the morning. Hugh, come help me. Derek, you too."

"Be right there," Derek said, forking in another bite. "Almost done."

He hurriedly ate, and watched as his father and brother left. His mother rose and picked up the soiled plates. Derek brought his to her and hesitated. "Ma?"

"What is it?" she asked.

Derek opened his mouth and then closed it. He couldn't do it. "Nothing," he said with a shrug.

He started to walk away, but his mother's light touch on his arm stopped him. "Now see here," she said. "You've never had secrets before; now's no time to start."

"I just was wondering," Derek said slowly, "here we're going to help the Elkins out. Matter of fact, we'd help just about anyone who needed it. Pa and Hugh were some of the first out there that night little Maddie was lost in the woods, and I bet we'll be plowing up the Elkins' land. So, why do we hate the Graysons so much and just as soon spit as look at them?"

His mother stared at him with a look he couldn't quite decipher. If he hadn't known better, he'd have thought he saw a hint of sorrow before his mother raised her brows and frowned at him. "Because they are Graysons," she told him. "That's enough."

"There's got to be another reason," Derek said. "The original reason. This has been going on for some time now. You and Pa got your reasons, and I remember Granny talking about it—pretty sure she cursed them her final breath—but I don't know why. Seems like I am getting left out of the reasoning. Reckon I just wondered. What with being an adult myself now."

His mother pressed her lips together as her eyes blazed. "Because that family's no good. Don't you know that?" She turned away, and Derek headed outside. There was no point in talking further.

No good. He'd heard that before. He knew the Graysons felt the same about his family. But why? Derek let out a sigh and pushed up his sleeves before taking his turn at the plow. Didn't really matter, did it?

Even if he got an answer, it didn't mean he'd find a solution. Wasn't nothing that was going to bring his family together with Ellen's. One thing he'd learned early on was nothing would make his pa change his mind about something once it was fixed on it. Which meant he'd never get to be with the woman he'd been thinking about since the first time he'd seen her.

Chapter 3

Ellen tried not to let her eyes linger on the Claytons, who were sitting two pews in front of her family, and to the left. She especially tried not to stare at Derek and fought her blush as she thought about the brazen way she'd kissed him. Each time she thought about it, she'd quickly defended herself. After all, he'd saved her life.

But that excuse led to nothing but incredible confusion as she wondered—not for the first time over the years—just why her parents hated his. Ellen let out a small sigh, and then guiltily looked down as her mother glanced at her. She knew the look her mother was giving her. *Pay attention.*

In the front of the church, Reverend Gabriel Sullivan was finishing his sermon. "When we turn the other cheek, my friends, when we forgive seventy times seven, we not only are looking after our fellow man, but we are healing our own hearts. I know how easy it is to let things upset us. How, when someone hurts our feelings or wrongs us, it's easy to hold a grudge."

All around her, Ellen heard murmurs of agreement. She reflected for a moment on the words. It was indeed easy. And, evidently, such a grudge could be held for generations. Two families here in town were testament to that.

The reverend spoke again, "But if we can learn to love one another, we actually find that we have more in common than we ever thought. Just as wonderful is we can break what has the potential to be a generational curse of hatred."

Ellen's eyes widened slightly. It almost sounded as though Reverend Sullivan was speaking right to her family and the Claytons. She was so distracted by the thought, she missed how he ended his sermon, only coming back to the present when the closing hymn began.

As their family filed out of the church building, she followed her mother over to their wagon. Her mother pulled out a covered basket with a loaf of bread, a good number of potatoes and carrots, and a jar each of butter and blackberry jam. Then she stopped and scowled. Ellen turned in the direction of the glare.

In the distance, she could see Mrs. Clayton holding two large covered baskets, and giving them to Mrs. Elkins. Mrs.

Elkins had tears running down her cheeks, and leaned in to hug Mrs. Clayton.

"Can you believe that woman?" Ellen's mother asked, exasperation clear in her voice.

"Which one?" Ellen asked, a little confused. She'd heard Mrs. Elkins was having a terrible time, which was why her mother had brought food, so she hoped that wasn't who her mother meant.

"Sadie Clayton, of course," her mother sniffed. "Look how she tries to outdo everyone! Two baskets! Humph! Well, I just hope whatever she brought doesn't kill the Elkins. I wouldn't eat a bite from a Clayton. As poisoned as they are, it would leach into the soil they grow in."

The words shouldn't have surprised Ellen, and in truth, they didn't. From the time she was a child, she remembered her parents talking that way about the Claytons. But she'd never felt that way herself. Mr. and Mrs. Clayton, though they ignored her, had never done anything to hurt her. She used to wonder if that was a good thing. Now, she wondered if there was some reason behind it. Like they were just waiting for the right time. The idea made her feel anxious.

As she watched her mother press her lips together and walk toward Mrs. Elkins to give her basket, Ellen replayed every interaction she could remember with the Claytons. They'd never seemed unkind to anyone else in the town.

But whenever her family neared, there was such tension in the air.

"Ellen! Stop daydreaming. Let's head home," her father said, climbing into the wagon. He muttered, "What are you wishing for now? To keep your parents waiting?"

Her cheeks crimson, Ellen realized her mother had returned, and quickly climbed into the wagon, sitting in the back. She didn't answer her father. Her daydreaming was a habit that irritated him. Wishing on nothing, he called it.

"That Sadie Clayton," her mother said as she settled herself. "She had the nerve to raise her eyebrows at my basket!"

"No manners," Ellen's father said. "But what can you expect from a Clayton?"

"Have they always been that bad?" Ellen asked.

"Always," her father answered.

She wanted to ask more, to see if her mother would add anything, but the tension in her mother's shoulders and the way her father was glaring at Mr. Clayton as they drove past made Ellen keep her mouth closed. She did look though, and her heart skipped a beat and made a tiny little flutter as Derek met her gaze.

As the wagon swayed gently and Ellen held to the sideboard, a wistful feeling came over her. What would it be like if she were allowed to feel that shiver of excitement without the guilt and fear of her parents' anger mixed in?

Near the Clayton wagon, she could see his parents glaring at hers. What had happened that made them so angry with the other?

The wagon shuddered suddenly, and Ellen's father shouted, "Woah!" as he stopped the horses.

"What's happening?" Ellen gasped, as she clutched the wagon's side.

"Don't know," her father said, jumping down. He looked at the wagon and groaned. "Wheel coming off. You two get out; I've got to fix this."

"While you do, I'll go talk to Maggie," Ellen's mother said. "I want to ask her something."

Ellen's father grunted, reaching for the bag of tools he kept in the wagon. This hadn't been the first time he'd needed tools while out, so oftentimes he brought a small bag with him when he went anywhere.

Ellen climbed down from the wagon and glanced around in case any of her friends were nearby to chat with for a few moments. She didn't see any of them, so she slowly started to walk toward the church garden. It would be close enough to see when the wagon was fixed, but far enough away that she could have a moment to herself without getting into a conversation she wasn't interested in.

Ellen stopped and smelled a deep purple iris, and then let her fingers trace its soft petals. The garden was maintained by several of the women in town, and she recognized this iris as being one Maggie from the diner grew.

She sat on the bench near a large tree and looked out over the church grounds, letting her gaze roam. People were talking in small groups, some were leaving in wagons or on foot, and a few children played quietly together. Her father was working on the wagon wheel, with one of the ranchers, Duncan, helping him. She wondered where Derek was. He was no longer with his parents, who were speaking with Dirk, the town's printer, and his wife Samantha.

"Looking for someone?" The rich voice made Ellen stiffen, and she glanced toward the tree. She could see just the smallest bit of Derek hiding behind it. Quickly, she looked away, not wanting to draw attention to him.

"Maybe," she said softly, so her voice wouldn't carry.

"I just wanted to make sure you were okay. After the other day," he told her.

"I am, thanks to you. If you hadn't come along when you did, I might not be here," Ellen said, remembering how dangerously close the snake had been.

"Can't have that," Derek said.

She glanced at him again, unsure what to say. "I wish...I wish I could see you a little better," she admitted.

"I'm worried someone might notice us together," Derek said, but he stepped closer to her.

"I wish it didn't matter," Ellen said, only a little surprised she said so. Where did this boldness come from when she spoke with him?

"Me too," Derek admitted. He moved a little closer and sat, his broad shoulders against the thick tree trunk. "You've got a lot of wishes," he said, and winked. "Glad I'm one of them."

It made her blush, and she fought to keep the smile off her face. She could look at him better now, and no one could see him so close to her, with him slunk down. "I reckon I do. Especially when it comes to you," she answered, surprising herself at her words.

Derek studied Ellen for a long moment, then said, "This is foolish. I shouldn't be here. It's dangerous. I don't want you in trouble because of me. And I'm not convinced yet that you aren't playing some sort of a trick on me."

But he didn't move away, and Ellen could hardly breathe. A trickle of pain filled her heart at his words. "Then why are you here?" she finally whispered.

"I can't seem to stop myself," he told her, his voice raw. "There's something about you. Draws me to you." His eyes hardened slightly. "Does that scare you? Me? A Clayton? So near? Is this a game to you?"

"Not at all," Ellen said. She raised her chin slightly, and then looked down at the ground, her cheeks flaming as the words released. "I'm not scared, and I can't stop thinking about you either. It's no game on my part. No trick either. That isn't the sort of person that I am."

From the corner of her eye, she saw him lift his hand slightly, and his fingertips brushed hers. "Then we've sure got a problem," he told her.

Ellen's eyes followed his hand as it left hers, then dragged her gaze to his. It was as though everything around them stopped. She was acutely aware of how close they were, and yet, how near everyone else was. This was no place nor time for the things she wanted to say or do. But, when would that moment come? Would it ever?

A heaviness had settled in the silence between them, and Derek's eyes were intense, nearly blazing as they bored through her. Ellen found herself lost in them, and didn't mind whatsoever. If this moment lasted forever, she'd never be without him.

"Time to go!" Ellen's father hollered suddenly.

She stood up quickly, but as she started to leave, Derek's hand grabbed hers. His touch nearly seared her, and she froze. Just as suddenly, his warmth was gone, and when she looked behind her, Derek was nowhere to be seen. Once again, he'd vanished.

Ellen pressed the hand he'd grabbed to her thudding heart as she hurried over to the family wagon. If only her father hadn't finished so soon. Who knew when she'd ever have such a moment again?

On the ride home, her parents talked and Ellen relived the moment she'd just had with Derek. The burning look in his eyes. How she'd wanted to kiss him again. That, more than anything, she longed to see him again.

Ellen made up her mind. She didn't care what happened. She was going to find a way to see Derek and spend time with him. Her heart would never belong to anyone else, she was sure of that.

It was obvious he was feeling something too. Though she didn't know him well, she could sense his honesty when he'd said how he felt. Ellen knew he wouldn't have been there, wouldn't have reached for her, if he wasn't wanting more.

And there was nothing, not even a generations-old feud, that would keep them apart if that was the case.

Chapter 4

The risk of talking to Ellen had been worth it. Especially when she had said the very thing Derek had hoped—that she had been thinking about him too.

Derek wasn't sure why he'd grabbed her hand, other than his fingers were acting of their own accord. He knew it was a bad idea. Dangerous. But he hadn't been lying. Something kept pulling him toward her, and he didn't want to fight whatever it was. He did want to keep it secret, though.

He'd meant what he'd said about not wanting her in trouble. He also didn't want his parents upset. This wasn't a good situation or a good idea, and he'd been right on that as well. How long would he and Ellen be able to sneak around before it was found out?

"And did you see Marta Grayson's face?" Derek's mother laughed as they rode home. "Just furious with me for bringing two baskets."

Derek wanted to say it wasn't about how much someone gave. It was that they were doing it for the right reason, which, he knew his parents—and likely Ellen's—had. But he also knew his parents would be delighted with the unexpected outcome for a few days. He wondered how often the Graysons talked about the Claytons. Were they always making jokes at their expense or comments the way his parents seemed to do?

When the laughter in the wagon died down, Hugh asked him, "Something on your mind?"

Derek shrugged. "Just thinking about the sermon, that's all."

"Which part?" his mother asked, turning so she could see him better. "We sure are blessed to have such a man of God here."

"The part about turning the other cheek," Derek said.

"Always do, always will," his father said with a nod. He barked out a laugh. "Unless it's a Grayson. Then it's an eye for an eye."

"Joe, not on a Sunday," his mother said, but Derek could see the corners of her lips twitching, and knew she didn't really mean it.

Stifling a sigh, Derek crossed his arms as he leaned against the back of the wagon. He absently reached for his pocket knife, and the soft wood he'd been carving into an animal, but remembered he'd left it at home. It would have been a good distraction. Taken him away from the feeling of unease starting to churn in his gut.

When he glanced at his brother, he saw Hugh shrug. Something inside him eased a little at the small motion. Was Hugh as much wanting to put all this aside like he was?

Derek had long suspected that his older brother didn't harbor quite the upset toward their neighbors that his parents did, but he had no way to confirm it. If he were wrong when he asked, he'd feel like a fool, and risk his father's anger.

He rode in silence on the way home while their parents talked, and as Derek took the horses to the barn, Hugh followed. "You better watch out," he said.

"Watch what?" Derek asked, loosening the harness.

"Being around Ellen Grayson," his brother said quietly.

Derek stiffened, and slowly brought his eyes to Hugh's. His older brother continued to keep his voice low as he said, "I saw you at church. Well, saw you walking away from her. I could tell you'd been talking."

"That so?" Derek asked, trying not to let on that his heart was pounding and fear was racing through his mind. Had Hugh told their parents? If not, would he?

His brother shrugged. "I don't care. I don't have no grudge against her or anyone else. But it's obvious our parents will never be friends with hers, so you'd better keep your distance. If not for your sake, then for hers."

"I know you're right," Derek said, and dropped the harness on a hook.

"But?" his brother asked.

Derek lowered his head a moment, then turned, meeting his brother's concerned expression. "I can't explain it," he said. "It's been growing for a while. And I can't seem to stop thinking about her. It doesn't matter. At night, in the morning, in the middle of the day. She just comes to my mind. Nothing I do gets her out of it."

"Maybe it's because she's like the tree in the Garden of Eden," Hugh said, a thoughtful expression growing on his face. "Forbidden fruit."

Derek thought about that for a moment. Was that it? He wasn't sure. Did he like Ellen only because he couldn't be with her? No, he didn't think that was what he was feeling drawn to. If that were the case, he wouldn't have felt so scared when he saw that snake after her. He wouldn't have felt that squeezing in his chest when he saw her sitting there on the bench in the church garden looking sad.

And, he most assuredly wouldn't have wanted to pull her into his arms and protect her from any and everything that might be upsetting her. Would he?

"I don't think that's it," Derek said finally. "It doesn't feel like that when I think about her."

"Then that's worrying," Hugh said, and crossed his arms. "If you've fallen in love with a Grayson, you'd better stop real quick before Pa and Ma find out."

"I know I should," Derek said. "But I'm twenty-three. Old enough to choose things for myself."

"Not and stay in the family," Hugh warned. "You know that."

"I do," Derek agreed. "I admit though, while I'm scared of them finding out, I'm more worried for her sake, not mine."

"You've got it bad," his brother said, shaking some oats into the horses' grain.

"Think you'll ever find a woman you like?" Derek asked. "You are a year older than me. You act like you know how I'm feeling, but I can't remember you ever saying there was someone you cared for."

He watched, feeling a little surprise as a look came over his brother's face he'd never seen before. It was somehow a combination of sadness and anger.

Before Derek could ask what his brother was thinking, Hugh answered. "Nope. Had one. They didn't like her. That's that. Maybe one day, but until then, I'm sure not looking."

"I...I didn't know," Derek said, squeezing his brother's shoulder. He felt badly for him. "Who was she?"

"Cara Hackland," Hugh said. "Was about two years ago. Turned out she was a distant cousin of the Graysons. Had no idea. Ma knew it though when I said her name."

"What happened?" Derek asked.

Hugh picked up a brush and started at the mare's neck. "Cara married someone else."

"The right one will come along," Derek said, even though his words felt hollow to him.

"If I told you that? About Ellen?" his brother asked.

Derek stilled. Shame raced through him. Of course those words were hollow. Only made his brother feel worse. "Yeah. You're right."

"If I can do it, so can you," his brother said with a sad smile. "Forget about her. Move on. Find someone else or don't, but whatever you decide to do, don't do it with a Grayson."

His brother's words were wise. Derek knew it. And, knowing now that his brother knew and even understood some of what he was feeling helped Derek in a way. Guilt washed over him. Here, his brother was just trying to warn him. But unlike Hugh, he didn't think he could just walk away.

Yet if he didn't, what kind of future could he give Ellen? A life on the run? There was no way his father would allow him to keep working the family land, and sure as anything, Ellen's pa wouldn't want him there. How would he provide for a wife? A future family? Would Ellen even want him if he had no assured future?

From outside the barn, their father called Hugh, and his older brother started toward the barn door. He stopped long enough to say, "Whatever you're planning, better not do it."

Derek raised an eyebrow. "What makes you so sure I'm doing anything but grooming the horse?"

"Because I know you, and for a short time, I had the same thought," his brother said as he walked away. "Then I realized it was pointless."

Derek didn't miss the slight sag to his brother's shoulders as he said the last. There was a lack of energy in Hugh's step. How hadn't he noticed sooner? He'd been so selfish. Hugh had been quieter for the last few years. At first, when Derek had noticed, his brother had snapped at him, told him to leave him be. As time had passed, he'd gotten used to Hugh being silent, working harder, and keeping to himself.

He realized now what that was. A part of Hugh's soul had likely died when he lost Cara. Cold chills washed over Derek, even though it was hot and humid in the barn. He didn't want that to be him. Didn't want to miss out on the spinning feeling in his stomach when he thought about Ellen, the way she made his pulse run, his mind come alive, his heart feel joy.

Derek swallowed hard, and then blew out a slow breath. He couldn't do it. Couldn't give Ellen up. He'd just have to figure out something. That was, if she was willing to risk losing her family as well. He didn't know, but Derek did know that all he wanted to do the rest of his life was love Ellen, with all of his being.

Chapter 5

Ellen froze, cocking her head to the side, the dish she'd been washing momentarily forgotten. Faintly, she could hear the clang, clang, clang of the church bell. Seeing as it wasn't Sunday, that could only mean one thing. Help was needed. Through the window, she spotted her father running, shouting and pointing. Her eyes turned upward to see smoke was filling the sky.

Fire.

Every hand would be needed. Ellen ran from the house, her mother right on her heels. She snatched two buckets on the way, and saw her father holding two as well. They raced to the town on foot, where, at a distance she could see lines were forming from the stream to the burning building. Smoke was thick and poured from the blacksmith's shop.

The roof was entirely in flames, and other buildings nearby were at risk. Even though the blacksmith's walls were made of stone as a precaution, sparks from the roof flew through the air, causing small smoldering spots in the grasses.

Wordlessly, she joined the others in one of several lines passing buckets to and from the stream and the blacksmith shop. The smoke stung Ellen's eyes. Even though she was about two hundred feet away, they watered. She could see several men trying to dig a firebreak between the blacksmith's shop and the building nearest it. Their shovels moved at a rapid pace, and she hoped it would be enough.

Ellen's arms ached, and her lungs burned, but she passed bucket after bucket. It was impossible to tell if it was making a difference. Thankfully, there was water in the stream. It wasn't always as deep this time of year.

More people had joined, and now there were four snaking lines of the bucket brigade, and two groups of people with shovels. A few people both older and younger than her dropped out, exhausted and unable to work further, but Ellen didn't dare. Every hand was needed. She'd work until she collapsed, and she wouldn't stop any sooner.

The person to her right staggered back, but someone took her place. Ellen passed the empty bucket, and when soot-stained hands brushed against hers, her eyes widened as a familiar tingle filled her.

"Fancy meeting you here," Derek said, passing her a filled bucket.

"Where there's smoke, there's a Clayton, my parents would say," Ellen answered, teasing as she grabbed it. "Seems they were right."

He barked out a cross between a cough from the smoke and a laugh. "My folks say something similar," he said, offering her the next bucket that had come to him. "Except about Graysons."

"Figures," she said, trying to hold back a giggle. She shouldn't be laughing at such a thing, but seeing him had given her both a small burst of energy, and a welcome distraction.

Ellen passed the bucket along the line, and then used her sleeve to wipe away the moisture from her face.

The fire was starting to reduce in size, but it was still so hot. Her dress clung to her in a most irritating way. She was incredibly thirsty and tired, but now she knew she wouldn't dare sit. Not while Derek was there. Who knew when she'd have a chance to see him again? Though the circumstances weren't good ones, Ellen planned to take advantage of the moment to be with him.

"Holding up?" he asked, shooting her a look she had trouble reading.

"Just fine," Ellen said. "You?"

He nodded. Exhaustion was evident on Derek's face. They didn't talk further, as it felt like too much work, just passed bucket after bucket. Ellen's arms were shaking now they were so tired. She longed to rest, but refused to quit.

Derek's face was concerned as he said, "You could stop. It's almost contained."

"I can't," Ellen said, even as her muscles screamed for relief and her lungs begged for clean air.

He didn't answer, likely understanding why she didn't want to pause. It was too important to help. The sooner it was done, the sooner everyone could rest. And, of course, there was the fact that if she did, she wouldn't get to spend this time with him. The flames were lower, nearly out. She was sure she could hold on a little longer. The bucket brigade had done it. They'd saved the rest of the town.

With a groan, Ellen dropped to the ground, like many others were doing. Children with ladles and buckets of switchel—water, vinegar, and molasses—walked down the bucket brigade lines, offering the cool and refreshing liquid. Ellen eagerly drank, then drank again.

A boy approached her with a bucket of water for anyone who wanted more, and Ellen used it to dampen her handkerchief. When she dabbed at her face, it came away nearly black.

A soft chuckle made her scowl. "What's so funny?"

"You made it worse," Derek said. "It's all smeared on you now. Want me to help?"

"I—"

"You get away from my daughter, Clayton," a harsh voice growled.

Ellen startled, and looked up to see her father, hands balled into fists. Derek's jaw tensed, but he nodded and stood without argument.

"Pa, he was just—" Ellen started.

"Leaving," her father said. "He's leaving. Surprised he's here. Thought Claytons were yellow bellied."

"No more than Graysons are," Mr. Clayton said, coming from behind Ellen's father. "How dare you speak to my son that way?"

"Your son was bothering my daughter," Ellen's father snapped.

"Pa—" Ellen tried again.

"Get to your ma," her father snarled. "It's for your own good."

Ellen felt a push from her father, and moved in that direction, but her eyes fell on Derek. He gave her a small shake of his head. She felt anger burning in her. Why was her father acting this way? She didn't blame Mr. Clayton at all. Her father was being rude.

"If my son was near your daughter, I'm sure he wasn't bothering her," she could hear Mr. Clayton say as she walked away. "Likely she was throwing herself at him, like a—"

He didn't get to finish. Ellen gasped at the comment, just as her father swung at the man. In the blink of an eye, there were men surrounding them, and Ellen saw Derek pulling his father back, while several others jumped between the men.

"That's enough!" Hank, who acted as the town's lawman, shouted. "Break it up! This isn't the time or the place."

There was a scuffling, and more shouting, but a moment later, fire in each man's eyes, Ellen's father and Derek's separated, and turned their backs to the other.

"How dare he speak that way," Ellen's mother said, coming up alongside of her. Then she added, "I'm shocked Sadie tolerates that."

It had been pointless to think for that half second that her mother was accusing her father of starting the problem, though Ellen knew that her father had started the argument. Had he always? Or did he and Mr. Clayton take turns?

"It's under control," her father said, shoving his hat lower on his head. "Time to leave."

Ellen glanced around as they walked back home. She wondered where Derek was. She didn't see his family anywhere around. Still, she didn't want to leave, on the off chance she could see him and apologize.

"Pa, could I catch up in a few moments?" she asked.

"What for?" her father asked gruffly.

"While I'm in town, I'd like to get a book," Ellen said, gesturing toward the diner that housed the town's library. "I know I'm a mess, but everyone is, and..." She bit her lip. "Never mind."

"Oh, let her go," Ellen's mother said. "It will show she's not the least bit bothered by those false accusations."

"Go ahead," her father said, though reluctantly. "I don't see any Claytons around."

"Don't take too long," her mother said. "Just in case."

Ellen nodded, and said, "I'm just going to wash my face and hands, then I'll go. I won't take long, I promise. I'll be home soon."

She hurried to the stream and wet her handkerchief multiple times until there were no more soot streaks on her face and hands. Rising from the bank of the water, she walked toward Maggie's café. There were a few people seated inside, now that the fire was out.

Ellen weaved through the tables over to the bookshelves that lined the back of the café. She quickly grabbed a book, hardly looking at the title, wrote her name and the title on the checkout sheet, and left again.

She couldn't explain it, but she felt a draw to return to the church garden. Ellen stopped at the edge of the church grounds. Should she? She ought to head home, like she'd promised. But... Ellen hesitated, torn between obedience and this strange longing she felt.

With a sigh, she turned to head home. She didn't want to upset her father, and she was tired. But as she did, she bumped into someone. Instinctively, she reached out and grabbed the person to keep from falling backward. "I'm s—"

The apology died on her lips when she saw Derek before her, her hands on his chest, and, somehow, his arms wrapped around her waist.

Chapter 6

"Hello," Derek said, looking down at Ellen who was in his arms and fit there perfectly. Her hands were pressed to him, and her fingers curled slightly into his shirt, as if trying to keep him there. Her expression of surprise quickly turned to embarrassment, then worry.

Derek understood. He released her and took a step back as she said, "I was hoping to see you."

"You were?" he asked.

"Yes. I...I want to apologize."

"For what?" Derek asked, wondering what in the world she'd have to apologize for.

"My father, and what he said to you. I don't know why he said that. Other than..." She stopped. And Derek understood why. It was one thing to know how her father spoke and talked about and thought of the Claytons. It was a whole other thing to say it. Especially to one's face.

"Actually, I'm also glad to see you. I wanted to apologize too, for what my father said." Derek glanced down, not surprised to see his hands had curled themselves into fists. "It made me right angry what he started to say, so I don't blame your father for it at all. I hope you know whatever was going to come out of his mouth was a lie. He's quick to temper."

"Do you know why they hate each other so much?" Ellen asked.

He shook his head. "I don't. Wish I did." He chuckled. "Your wishing habit seems to be wearing off on me."

Ellen gave a soft laugh. "I reckon I do wish things a lot." She sighed, then shrugged. "I don't know either. It's frustrating because, well, I saw your parents Sunday. They seem like good people, overall."

"They are," Derek said earnestly. "Give you the shirt off their backs. Unless..."

"Unless it's to a Grayson," Ellen said wryly.

"Yeah." Derek crossed his arms. "I don't know what to do about it. Whatever this grudge is about has been going on a long time. Maybe even a hundred years, if it's on its third generation."

"I guess that means we have to hate each other too," Ellen said.

"I can tell you what I'd hate," Derek said, taking a half step closer.

Ellen didn't move, though she did take a quick glance around, and then reached her hand out to pull him closer to a large tree to block them better. "Tell me," she said.

"Not getting to see you," Derek told her. "Not getting to talk to you."

"I would hate that too," Ellen said softly.

They were so close, all Derek would have to do was to lean down and he could kiss her, but he stopped himself, not wanting to take advantage of her, and not wanting to scare her either.

"You know," Derek said, shoving his hands into his pockets so that he didn't end up grabbing her and holding her tightly, "just because they don't get along doesn't mean we have to be that way. Together, maybe, we could change things. You know, so the next generation doesn't hate the other."

"You mean, be friends?" she asked, tipping her head slightly to the side as she studied him.

"Sure, friends," he said, though he wanted so much more. It didn't matter, though; more wasn't going to happen. Even being friends was dangerous.

A strange tension filled the air. All around them, it felt heavy. Hard to breathe. Derek was sure it wasn't from the smoke that still lingered. It was from how Ellen was looking at him. In a considering way, as though she were thinking carefully about what he'd said, and forming her answer. He wondered what was going through her mind, and what she'd say. If it was something he even wanted to know.

"Just friends?" Ellen asked, and he felt his heart speed up.

"I'd be anything you wanted me to be," Derek told her honestly. "If I thought it would make you happy."

A flush spread across Ellen's cheeks, and she reached down, touching his arm. Derek pulled his hands from his pockets, and took her hands gently into his. He didn't speak, though. His chest had tightened up so much, he couldn't seem to squeeze any words out.

"Being with you makes me happy," Ellen told him quietly. "In whatever way I can have. When...when do you think we can see each other again?"

"I don't know. But—Wait. I am coming to town tomorrow for supplies. Around one. Think you could meet me here?"

Ellen nodded. "I think so. I borrowed a book. I'll tell Ma I wanted to get another. Or offer to run an errand since I'll get all my chores done early."

The sound of someone walking near them made him tense, and a quick glance showed Ellen doing the same. "I need to go," she said. "I said I wouldn't be long. But, tomorrow." She gave him a shy smile.

"Tomorrow," he echoed, stepping further away from her.

Derek watched as Ellen hurried away, the book she'd been holding clutched to her chest. He saw her quickly look over her shoulder before she turned forward again, her walk as fast as her legs could carry her without a run.

Derek could hardly believe what had just happened. Had he and Ellen agreed to meet up? To become friends? Or more? If they did, could the feud between their families die with him?

There wasn't enough time in the world to sort out his thoughts, to figure out what he was going to do. There was only one thing important to him. Protecting Ellen. What he was doing was dangerous, and he didn't want her to pay the price. Was he being selfish right now? He likely was. But he also didn't want to not explore whatever this thing was with her.

"There you are. Ready to head home?" Hugh asked, coming toward him.

"Sure am. Glad we happened to be here in town," Derek said, hoping that Hugh hadn't seen Ellen. After their conversation the other day, he didn't want Hugh thinking he was ignoring his—admittedly good—advice.

"Me too. The blacksmith says he doesn't need anything, and a few men have already offered to help rebuild the roof. But, I'm sure the reverend will let us know if he changes his mind and needs us."

Derek nodded, following Hugh over to the wagon, where they'd brought in a load of firewood to the Elkins just a short time before. He squinted at his reflection in a glass window. So much had happened in the last few hours, he felt as though he should look different. He felt different. Could anyone tell? He hoped not.

Derek didn't want to answer questions or make excuses. He also didn't like how he had to hide that he cared for Ellen. That being with her meant more to him than anything else.

He also wished that he didn't have this worrying feeling looming over his head. One of disaster waiting to happen. Maybe Hugh was right. He should walk away while he still could.

Chapter 7

Ellen smoothed her skirt, then tugged at it again. There were no wrinkles and it hadn't pulled up; she just felt nervous. What if Derek didn't show up? She wasn't sure how long she could stay here. Especially without anyone asking why she was there.

All night she'd tossed and turned, a confusing mixture of excitement and terror filling her. She knew the trouble she'd be in if anyone discovered her and Derek. Not to mention what might happen to him. But she was also looking forward to seeing the person who'd been on her mind.

Would he get there soon? Or had he changed his mind? Ellen found herself filled with a restless energy. It took all she had in her not to jump up and pace or twist her hands, but she knew if she stood, she'd be more visible. Here, in this small nook of the church garden, she was covered on three sides by neatly trimmed shrubbery. The sun hit the large tree just so, casting a shadow over the garden area.

The tip of Ellen's boot twisted back and forth in the pebbled walkway. She'd always liked its soft crunching sound as she stepped on it. Her eyes swept the nearby area while she waited. Some birds fluttering their wings, a rabbit hopping past, but no humans.

No Derek.

She tried not to let that worry her. Make her feel a fool for waiting for him. *Eagerly* waiting for him. After all, he'd said he had to pick up supplies. Surely, he wasn't playing a trick on her.

Ellen tried to ignore her mother's voice that rolled around in her mind, saying what could you expect from a Clayton but dishonesty?

A scuffing sound from the walkway set her heart pounding. Ellen couldn't see who it was. Hopefully not the reverend or his wife. Not that she minded talking to them. It's just that today, her heart and mind and focus were on one thing. Her meeting with Derek.

She also didn't want to risk Derek not coming if someone else was there, a person who might tell her parents or his that he had been.

Ellen's eyes landed on the newcomer. Hat low, there he was, and Ellen stood quickly. "Hello," she said softly. Shyly.

"I hope I didn't keep you waiting," he said, taking his hat off and holding it tightly. "Forgot the list and had to turn around to get it."

"I've done that myself," Ellen said with a laugh.

"Something we have in common then," he said, sitting near her on the bench. Derek let out a breath and shook his head. "I admit. I was afraid you might not be here."

"I was worried about the same," Ellen confessed. "But I'm so glad you are."

They sat in silence. It felt a little awkward. As if they each weren't sure what to do or say. Ellen tried to summon the courage to speak, to perhaps say something to erase the tension she was feeling. Her mind drew a blank, though. The singular thought forming in her mind was, had this been a mistake? Agreeing to meet him?

Derek cleared his throat, and Ellen's eyes shot to his. "Would it be okay if I held your hand?" he asked.

Ellen nodded shyly, but as soon as his fingers were wrapped around hers, the awkwardness fled, and she relaxed. Derek appeared to as well.

"My order will be ready in about an hour," he told her. "Can you stay that long?"

"I can," Ellen said with a nod. "I already chose a book from the café." She held up a dime novel with her free hand.

Derek took it from her. "I read this one. It's got a real good ending."

"I'm glad to hear that." Ellen set the book alongside her again. "Have you ever read—"

The faint sound of voices sent the two of them to opposite ends of the bench, no longer holding hands. Ellen held her breath, unsure whether she should flee or hold still. They waited a moment uncertainly, but when no one appeared, they hesitantly moved closer again, though Ellen kept her hands in her lap, while Derek toyed with his hat.

This was no way to have a friendship, or anything else. Ellen's gaze fell into her lap, and she tried to stop the quivering of her lips. Of all the things she'd done in her life, pretending she wasn't falling for Derek was the hardest.

"I'm sorry," Derek said suddenly. "This sure isn't fair. It's a bad idea too."

"It's not fair," Ellen agreed, ignoring his comment about it being a bad idea. She met his eyes. "Not to you or me. If only we could fix things. Make our parents get along again."

"That'd be great," Derek said, "but I don't see how it could happen. Not since it's been going on for so long."

"Maybe I can figure out why they don't like each other," Ellen said, a spark of hope building. "There's got to be someone around here who knows why."

"Who's the oldest person in town?" Derek asked. "That's a place to start maybe. But I don't know." Doubt filled his voice. "Maybe you shouldn't. If you go around asking questions, it might get back to your parents. I don't want you to get in trouble. Especially not because of me."

"Then I'll be careful," Ellen said. "But I want to know. If for no other reason, I'm curious. What could be so terrible that for decades two families have hated each other so much?"

"It's a good question," Derek agreed. "I'd like it to stop with us. If possible."

"So would I," Ellen said.

They sat quietly for a moment, until Derek said, "I'm kind of glad for that snake. Gave me a chance to talk to you."

"You did more than that," Ellen reminded him. "You saved my life."

"I couldn't let anything happen to you," Derek said, reaching for her hand again.

Ellen inched closer. "Can I ask you something? Promise you won't get mad at me."

"I'd never be mad at you," Derek said. "Ask me anything."

She swallowed hard. "Did it go through your mind, even for a second, to turn away? Pretend you didn't see me? Because I'm a Grayson?"

"Never." Derek's voice was firm, and he reached over to raise her chin slightly from where it had drooped as she looked down into her lap.

Ellen's eyes searched his, but before she could say anything, Derek was speaking again.

"I'll tell you what went through my mind. Fear. Fear I would miss or hit you. Fear I wasn't in time. That the woman I can't stop thinking about might die before my eyes. You don't know this, you couldn't, but for years I've thought about you. From the first time I saw you, your hair in long braids when you were singing while you picked wildflowers. Each time I saw you, my heart started thumping, and I couldn't wait until the next time I saw you again. Even if I knew nothing could come of it."

"I noticed you too," Ellen said. "And...well, I admit. Each time there's a pie or picnic auction, I'm always real grateful that you didn't bid on anyone."

"I've been worried about that too," Derek chuckled. "Didn't want to see someone with you. The very idea makes my heart hurt. That's why I buy my pie slices from Carissa. She's already got someone."

Ellen moved closer, and sighed. Their knees were now touching. "Now that I know, I wish there was one soon. And I wish you could bid on my pie or my basket. And we could sit together, and our parents wouldn't say anything."

"That's a lot of wishes," Derek said, a sigh in his voice too. "None of that's likely, but it sure would be nice."

"Ma says I wish too much," Ellen said.

"Nah," Derek told her. "Not at all. Wishing is a good thing. It's putting it out in the world. Sort of like a goal. Sets your intention." When Ellen looked at him, eyes wide, Derek shrugged. "Least, that's what I read in a book."

"I'm glad you like to read," Ellen told him. Then she sat up suddenly. "I've had an idea. Maybe we could pass notes to each other. Inside of the books at the library. If you go there anyway, it wouldn't look strange you opening a couple of them to browse inside."

Derek grinned at her. "I like that idea. But which ones?"

Ellen pursed her lips in thought. "I'll leave my notes to you in books where the author starts with a D. You leave yours in an author that starts with E. Look for the ones that no one ever really checks out. Let's do page twenty-five. So that no one knows it's us, and just in case the letters are found, we'll just sign them E and D."

"That's a good plan," he told her, admiration in his voice.

"As much as I'd love to take credit for it, I read it in a book," Ellen admitted with a laugh.

Derek squeezed her hands gently. "I have to go. The order is ready I bet. But I'm going to write you tonight."

Ellen whispered, "I'll do the same. I wish you didn't have to go. That I didn't have to go."

She stood, and Derek stood with her. They faced each other, a strong magnetic pull drawing her close to him.

His hands came to her waist, and Ellen tipped her head upward. Was Derek about to kiss her?

Just as his head lowered, there was the barking of a nearby dog, then the sound of someone calling out to it, just on the other side of the bushes. Derek stepped back, and before Ellen could blink, he'd vanished.

"How does he do that?" she wondered, then realized she'd whispered the question.

Quickly, she picked up the book and headed in the direction of home. She knew she couldn't ask to visit the town library again for another few days, but nothing could stop her from writing Derek a note for when she did go.

It wasn't much, and it wasn't as good as seeing him in person, but it would be something, and she couldn't wait for her first note from him. To have a piece of Derek she could hold, forever.

Chapter 8

Derek nodded at Maggie as he walked into the café. "Welcome. Here for a bite?" she asked.

"Could I get three of those ginger cookies?" he asked. "I'll take them with me for the ride home."

Maggie set to getting his cookies, and Derek strolled casually toward the books in the back of the café. At least, he hoped it looked casual. It was about all he could do not to rush right away to the books written by an E author. He was glad that he'd been a frequent visitor of the town library since it started. Otherwise, it might look real strange him coming in so often.

He flipped through a book about farming, and another on knots. Then he went toward the E's, and grabbed a history book, quickly flipping to page 25. Nothing. He tried another E book, one on animals, and was rewarded with a neatly folded square on page 25. He slid it into the dime novel he really wanted, and strode back to Maggie, who'd set his cookies on the counter in a bit of brown paper.

"Pa also wants to know if he can order a cherry cheese pie and a blackberry pie," Derek said. "He wants to keep them secret for Ma's birthday next week."

"What day do you need them?" Maggie asked, pulling out a piece of paper.

"Tuesday," Derek said. "But I can get them Monday too."

"We've a quilting bee Monday afternoon at the church," Maggie said, tapping the pencil on the counter. "If you come then, your mother might not see you sneak them home."

"Then that's what I'll do," Derek said, also glad for the information that Monday might not be a good day to meet with Ellen with so many women around the church.

It had been a week since they'd last been together for an hour. This time, he'd brought some harnesses into town to be repaired, while she was taking some eggs and butter to the bakery. They'd only had a short time, but it was enough to hold him over until they could have longer.

Almost.

The truth was, until Ellen was assuredly his, and in his arms without fear of looking over his shoulder or hers, he'd feel a hollow in him each time they were apart.

Climbing back into the wagon, Derek started home. Sacks of flour from the mill—and his excuse for coming to town—rested in the back. He bit into one of the cookies, and eagerly unfolded the letter. The horses knew the way, so he turned his focus to Ellen.

Dearest D,

My heart longs for you. What little time I've seen you is not enough, could never be enough.

If you should see this, I'll be doing the shopping Thursday.
E

Thursday. That was tomorrow. Derek wasn't sure he'd have an excuse to come back into town before Sunday. He knew he'd try, though. Even if he just could exchange hellos while she was shopping...but no. He couldn't. A Clayton never said hello to a Grayson.

Maybe he could pretend to bump into her. Then ignore her. That might work. Or, what would buy him more time, knock into her while she was carrying her groceries. Then help her pick them up. He'd be able to reach for something at the same time as her, brush her hand.

No. A Clayton wouldn't help a Grayson, not even with picking up something they dropped. He had to stop thinking things could ever be normal between them or their families.

Derek swallowed. This whole thing had been much harder than he ever imagined. So far, however, they'd kept their acquaintance a secret. He hated it though. Hated pretending he didn't know her. Didn't like her. Nothing could be further from the truth.

His house was coming into view. Derek hurriedly folded the note and stuck it in his pocket. This one made the second from her. He'd place it with the first message, inside of the chest at the foot of his bed, inside of a small box he'd made years before that had a little lock on it.

As Derek drew closer, he could see his mother standing outside, wildly gesturing with her arms and stalking back and forth a few steps this way, and then that. He frowned. Was something the matter? He urged the horses to go faster. Hugh had joined her now, and was pointing to the barn. His mother stalked off in that direction.

"What's going on?" Derek asked, pulling up. "Something wrong?"

"Ma's upset because of the Graysons," Hugh said.

"What'd they do?" he asked.

Hugh shrugged.

"I'll tell you," Derek's mother said, coming closer. "They gave the Elkins two chickens. When they knew we were going to do that."

"Then, they'll have four," Derek said. "Seems a better number. Anyway, maybe they didn't know."

"That's not the point," his mother said, exasperated. "They gave them first. Now, we either have to give more or something else. Why do they always try to outdo us?" She stormed away.

"I'm not sure I'm following," Derek said slowly.

"I know I'm not," Hugh agreed. "Let me help with the flour."

Between them, they got the sacks into the cellar, and Derek worked for two hours in the field. Over dinner that night, he listened as his mother complained about the chickens, and his father talked about giving a cow who had a few years left. Hugh was quiet, a vacant expression on his face, and Derek wondered if he stayed here for the rest of his life, would that happen to him? Or was that the look he'd wear when reality took over and proved he couldn't be with Ellen? The idea was discouraging.

"Pa," Derek offered, "if you are going to give a cow or anything else, I'll be happy to take it to town Thursday for you."

"You've been offering to go to town a lot," his father said. "Any particular reason?"

"No, not really," Derek said.

"Come on now, what's her name?" his mother asked.

Derek dropped his fork he was so flustered, while his parents laughed. He didn't miss Hugh's sympathetic look, and perhaps that was worse. "Not anybody," he said. "You know that."

"Sure, sure," his father said. Then he shook his head. "No, I need you here Thursday. Got to finish those fence repairs."

Derek nodded, swallowing down his disappointment with a bite of fried potato. His mother stood and brought over a cobbler she'd made, and though it was his favorite—strawberry—Derek was having trouble paying attention.

His folks thought he was interested in someone. That wasn't good. In fact, it was terrible. What if they discovered it was Ellen? Had he given himself away? It wasn't like he even got to see her much. Did they need to stop altogether?

"Thanks for dinner, Ma," Derek said a short time later. "I'll get started on the milking."

He headed toward the barn, hoping to be alone with his thoughts. He could hear Hugh chopping wood, and his father checking one more time on the horses. Frustration filled him, and Derek closed his eyes for a moment as he milked. Behind his lids he saw Ellen. He couldn't give her up. But how was he going to be able to see her? Especially if now his parents were watching his every move, thinking he was interested in someone?

Derek sighed. Maybe Ellen was right, and the best way would be to figure out why their parents hated each other, and try and change it. It didn't matter if the idea worried him. Something had to be done. If nothing else, maybe they'd learn that nothing could be changed. He wondered if she'd been asking around. Tonight, when he wrote her, he'd ask. If he could figure out a way to word it in a way that no one would know if they stumbled across the note.

Then, he'd just have to wait for an answer, and hope he could slip away into town before too long. If only there was some other way to go about without sneaking around and risking getting caught. But there wasn't.

Chapter 9

Happily, Ellen tucked the note Derek had left her inside of a book into the trunk where she had a few of her childhood things, like the rag doll her mother had made her, a handful of ribbons, and some button necklaces. All nostalgic things, and no reason for anyone to go poking about through them.

If only she could hear him speak the sweet words in his note. He had written, *I count the minutes until I can see you again. How is it that I find myself thinking of you every moment?*

It was incredibly romantic, and his words echoed the ones that Ellen felt herself. Of course, her practical side had to go and spoil it for her at times. Like now, when it reminded her that this was pointless. There was no way at all she and Derek would ever be able to be together.

No, what would happen instead, was he'd marry someone else, and her heart would shatter. Not break, but shatter. Completely, utterly, irreparably.

Ellen drew in a shuddering breath. She couldn't think like that. She had to hope. It was the only way. Surely there was something she could do about this.

"Ellen!" her mother called.

"I'm coming!" she replied, and hurried out of her room and into the kitchen where her mother was sitting at the table.

"Did you need me?" Ellen asked.

"Yes. I've a terrible headache, and I promised the dressmaker I'd drop off the lace I'd made her. Would you please do that for me?"

A chance to go to town? To hide her newest note into a book and check for one from Derek? Of course she would.

"Yes, right away," Ellen said. "Where is it?"

"In the basket near the front door," her mother said.

"Can I get you anything before I go?" Ellen asked. "A cool towel for your head?"

"No, no, I'm going to lie down for a little," her mother said, rubbing at her forehead. "There's no rush to return."

No rush. That was even better. Perhaps Ellen would run into Derek. Or...or perhaps she might have the chance to ask someone if they knew anything about the feud between her family and his. After all, if she didn't know what it was about, she couldn't try and mend whatever was broken between their families.

Even though Ellen sensed that Derek was apprehensive about her doing such a thing, she knew she'd be careful. Besides, wording it as simply being curious wasn't likely to bring much attention to her. If her parents did find out, she'd simply tell them the subject had come up, and she'd asked what the others knew.

"You rest," Ellen said, realizing she needed to answer her mother. "I'll be sure not to shut the door loudly when I leave."

She returned to her room to get her hat, and a few moments later was walking toward town. As she approached, her eyes fell, as they always did, to the large tree in the middle of Deepwater. Its branches were wide and full, and the tree was older than the town.

Deepwater had a good number of shops and businesses. It seemed every year a new family arrived or a new place was built. They were quite respectable too. There wasn't just the church and school and the post office. There were now two general good stores, the dressmaker, a tailor, a print shop, a shoemaker, a blacksmith—who just had his new roof put on—and several other places.

Of course, her favorite was the café, with its library, and not just because Derek slipped notes there for her. No, it was a lovely place to enjoy a mug of cider and a sweet or a meal. Maggie had come to Deepwater with Hank, when the town was next to nothing, and they had practically become founding business members. They had—

Practically been founding members. Did that mean Maggie, who knew just about everything about everyone, would know why the Claytons and the Graysons didn't get along? It was possible, and even though Maggie was a bit of a gossip, she was also the kind of person not to say anything, if you asked her not to.

Perhaps she'd be able to learn something at the café. The idea put purpose into Ellen's step, and she hurried toward the building. At the last moment, she remembered the lace she was supposed to deliver, and went into the dressmaker's shop.

As the small bell tinkled when she walked in, Ellen's eyes landed on a lovely green fabric the color of the pears in their orchard, and went right to it.

"Beautiful, isn't it?" the dressmaker asked.

"Yes," Ellen said. "I wish I had the money for it. I'm not quite sure I do."

"I can hold it for you for a week, if you'd like?" the woman offered. "Just in case?"

"I'd love that," Ellen said. "I will count my money when I get home. In the meantime, here is the lace for you. Ma has an awful headache, so I brought it for her."

The dressmaker peeked into the basket, then pulled out one of the lace cuffs. "Oh, that's lovely. Do tell your mother I said so. And, here." The dressmaker handed

Ellen an envelope with the money for the lace pieces, then removed the lace from the basket.

"Thank you," Ellen said, tucking it into the now empty basket. "I'll let you know on the fabric."

She left, the door's soft chime sounding again, and headed toward the café. The reverend was inside at the counter, as was Maggie. Ellen's heart leaped. This was perfect. She could speak to them both.

Hesitantly, not wanting to interrupt their conversation, Ellen approached.

"Hello," Gabriel said, smiling at her. "Isn't it a wonderful day?"

"It is," Ellen said. "It's perfect outside." She looked between the reverend and Maggie. "I'm so glad you are both here. I had a question, and hoped one of you might know the answer."

"What is it?" Maggie asked.

"It's...it's rather delicate," Ellen admitted. "So, I'd be grateful for you to keep it to yourselves." At their nods, she continued. "I'm sure you have noticed that my family doesn't get along well with the Claytons."

"Huh! And here I always thought those daggers your folks shot at each other were the friendly kind," Maggie said with a chuckle.

"Now that you mention it..." Gabriel said. Then he sighed. "I've been trying to hint to your father it might be time to let bygones be bygones."

"That's just it," Ellen said, "and what I wanted to ask you. I don't know what they are so upset about. In fact, I'm not sure they do either. Only that it's been going on for generations, and they don't plan to stop. Do you know why our two families don't get along?"

To her disappointment, both the reverend and Maggie shook their heads.

"It was that way when we arrived," Maggie said.

As Ellen's eyes went to Gabriel, he said, "Yes, it's true. But there is someone who might know."

"Who?" she asked.

"Peter. His father and his father's father were both here in this town serving as postmaster." Gabriel shrugged. "It's possible he might know. I don't think any other family has been around as long as his. Well, other than you Graysons and Claytons."

"Then I will seek him out," Ellen said. "Thank you."

"Now, can I get you anything to go along with that book I'm suspecting you are going to get?" Maggie asked.

"Yes. Two sugar cookies," Ellen said. "Please."

While the reverend waved goodbye and left, Ellen paid for the cookies, slipped them into her basket to enjoy on the way home, and went to the bookshelves. Through one of the windows she could see the post office. It was open, though there was a long line snaking around the building, but now that she knew Peter might have an answer, she was determined to ask.

Perhaps he could help her put a stop to this feud between her parents and Derek's. If that could happen, there would be no reason why she and Derek couldn't be friends. Or more. But what would happen if Peter didn't know? Who could she ask? Or should she just give up? Just by mentioning it to the reverend and Maggie, word might get around, even if they'd promised to keep quiet. What would happen if her parents knew she was making inquiries? She wasn't sure how they'd react, but Ellen also knew she didn't want to find out.

She had let herself do the unthinkable, get close to a Clayton. But it hadn't been a bad thing. Opposite, actually. And Ellen couldn't imagine being without him. Didn't want to be without him.

Her heart dropped, falling all the way down into her stomach where it sat there churning. She'd gotten herself into a fine mess. Was there any hope of fixing it?

Chapter 10

Derek had to stop himself from pacing. Ellen had left him a note that she was able to meet for a short time today in their spot. Dusk was approaching. They'd never met so late, and something about that made their clandestine meeting feel even more forbidden than it already was.

He'd been waiting a half hour, and hoped she hadn't changed her mind.

Derek had been thinking. He wanted to pledge his love to Ellen. It wasn't much, and not what she deserved, but he'd carved her a small heart out of a piece of cherry wood. It was small enough to close her fingers around as it rested in her palm. The perfect size to keep secret, but still remind her he was thinking of her.

If she came today, that was.

Derek reached inside his shirt pocket to check the wood carving was there when he heard the soft crunching of the walkway. A moment later, Ellen appeared, slightly out of breath.

"I'm so sorry," she said. "At the last moment, I couldn't get away. It feels like all week has been like that. I couldn't even speak with Peter the day before yesterday because Pa saw me and sent me home."

"Peter? The postmaster?" Derek asked.

"Yes. Reverend Sullivan and Maggie thought if anyone would know why our parents didn't get along, it might be him."

"I don't know," Derek said, doubt filling him. He knew Ellen had mentioned trying to find out why their parents didn't like each other, but he hadn't realized she'd go around talking to everyone. He knew for a fact that Maggie was frequently the source for "news." What would she think about Ellen asking questions? Or say? Perhaps the correct question was, say to whom?

"Peter is not much older than us," he added, hoping she wouldn't take his pause of silence for upset. "I'm not sure what he'd know."

"His family has been here longer than any other," Ellen said. "That's what I was told anyway." Then she hesitated. "Do you mind my asking him?"

Did he? Derek thought over the question. "I don't," he finally said. "Just what if it gets back to your folks you were talking to him?"

"I worried about that after I asked Maggie and the reverend, but why would anyone suspect anything more than curiosity?" Ellen said.

"I don't know. I hope they wouldn't. I'm just nervous, I guess. That's all," Derek said.

"I am too, but if it's the only way I have a chance to get to be with you, without always hiding around, I'm willing to do it," Ellen said.

"I'm willing too," Derek said. It was true. Guilt flooded him over the fear he'd felt a moment before. Here he was, wanting to pledge his affection, and he was letting fear of his parents and hers take that away from him. He hadn't realized Ellen was so bold, and it made him like her all the more. It also made him feel a little bit bad that she was willing to get to the bottom of things, and here he was, scared to do it.

She sat on the bench, and Derek joined her. "I have something for you," he told her, anxious to take his mind off his shortcomings. "I hope you'll like it." He reached into his pocket and then pulled out the small wooden heart. He hid it in his fist, and said, "Close your eyes."

Ellen did, but then cracked one eye open. The way she squinted at him was adorable, and he longed to kiss her. "I just remembered something," she said.

"What?" Derek asked.

"Last time you asked me to close my eyes because you wanted to give me something, you dropped a hairy spider on me."

Derek stared at her in shock, and then let out a laugh. "I'd forgotten about that! How old were we? Six? Seven?"

"I was furious," Ellen said. "That's all I remember. Well, and scared. It was huge."

"I'm sorry," Derek said, even though he could still feel the laughter bubbling up in him. "I promise, this time it's nothing creepy. It's something I made. And I hope you'll like it."

"I'm trusting you," Ellen said, giving him a warning look before she closed her eyes and timidly opened her hands in her lap.

Derek couldn't stop the grin as he remembered all those years before she'd done the same, and he'd played the prank. Why had he done it? Likely because he was a kid, and she was a Grayson. And...because she'd been there, her long, auburn hair in curls and looking so pretty. He'd wanted to get close to her.

Too bad that was the only way he knew how. Of course, his parents had thought it hilarious.

Derek set the heart in Ellen's hand, and then slowly dragged his fingers across her wrist. He didn't miss her sharp inhale as he stroked her skin. "Go ahead," he said, his voice low. "Open your eyes."

Her long lashes fluttered open, and Ellen gasped as she saw the heart. "Oh! Did you make this?"

"I did," Derek told her, pleased she seemed to like it.

"It's perfect," she said, holding it close and then pressing her lips to it. Derek couldn't take his eyes off of her. "Thank you. I-I wish I had something to give you."

"I don't need anything but you," Derek told her honestly. "I don't want anything but you."

"That's what you have," Ellen answered, moving closer to him. "You have my heart as well, and all my thoughts are of you. Every breath I draw is for you, and every moment of time I wish I were with you."

"Oh, Ellen," Derek said, his voice rough. He brought his hands back to hers. "I wish we didn't have to hide. I can't shake this feeling we're going to get caught, and I'll lose you. Or you'll get taken away. I feel like such a coward. Here you are, looking for answers. Here I am, scared this is a bad idea." Derek dropped his head into his hands.

"You won't lose me," Ellen said passionately as she squeezed his hand. "I don't want to be with anyone but you."

"You say that," Derek said softly, "and I know it's true. But what if you don't get a choice?"

"Then I'll spend my life loving you, anyway. Even if you aren't with me." Tears welled up in Ellen's eyes, and Derek hastened to wipe them as they spilled onto her cheeks.

"I didn't mean to make you cry," he said. "Honest. I'm just worried, is all."

"I know," Ellen whispered. "I am too. That's why I wanted to learn more. See if I could fix things between our folks."

"There's nothing to fix." Derek startled as his brother's voice broke into the conversation. He scrambled to his feet, putting himself between Hugh and Ellen.

"Relax. I'm not going to hurt her," Hugh said, as he looked at Ellen, then turned his attention back to his brother. "But I've got a warning for you both. I'm not going to tell our parents, but you both better quit this before it goes any further. Say goodbye. You know this won't end well. Not for either of you. It's best to spare yourself heartache, and before it's too late."

Ellen's eyes were wide, and she was trembling. Derek wrapped an arm around her, and pleaded with Hugh, "I can't."

His brother just looked at him sadly. "You don't have a choice and I know you know that."

Hugh turned and walked away, and Derek said hastily, "I have to go. I don't think he'll tell our folks, but..."

"Go," Ellen said. She gave him a smile that didn't quite meet her eyes. "I love you." She pressed her lips to his cheek, but stepped back far too quickly for him to turn his head and put his lips on hers.

"I love you, Ellen," Derek said, and then left her, racing after his brother and hoping against hope that Hugh wasn't lying, and wouldn't tell their parents about him and Ellen. He'd been worried about someone finding out, and now, they had.

Chapter 11

"Are you feeling unwell?" Ellen's mother asked, looking up from the cinnamon roll dough she was mixing.

"I'm fine, Ma. Just...I don't know. Tired, I guess." Ellen gave as bright of a smile as she could muster, and turned her attention back to the breakfast dishes.

Tired wasn't a lie. She'd hardly slept for worry since she last saw Derek. She kept reliving the moment his older brother had appeared. Kept trying to dissect each micro expression on his face, each word he'd said. That had been four days ago, and she'd not been able to get into town. The next time she could, Ellen had a letter to put inside of a book for Derek.

"Are you too tired to go into town for me?" Ellen's mother asked. "It would be just my luck to go and run into that Sadie Clayton or her husband. I'm still quite steamed about her having the audacity to offer me her old shawl when she saw me without one Sunday."

"I'm happy to do it," Ellen assured her mother. "With any luck, I won't run into her."

"Or any other Clayton," her mother muttered. "One's as bad as another."

"Are they all?" Ellen asked, unable to stop herself. She didn't think Derek was. Quickly, she said, "I don't remember the other Claytons before them. Mr. Clayton's parents. Were they awful too?"

Ellen's mother hesitated. "That's a question for your father," she finally said. "I don't rightly know. Or recall."

"That's right, you married into the Graysons. Was there this feud when you were growing up too?" Ellen asked.

"There was. But no one talked about it. They, and then Sadie and I, kept our distance from each other." Ellen's mother quietly added, "I knew Sadie, before."

"Before she got married to a Clayton? Was she nice?" Ellen asked. She was surprised her mother was talking so much, and hoped maybe she'd learn something useful, both now and when she went into town.

"She was just...Sadie," Ellen's mother said softly. "That's all." She plunged her hands into the dough, and her voice wobbled slightly as she said, "I need you to take that lace to the dressmaker, and get me a new tin of tea, and a pound of sugar for my jam I'm making. Actually, make it two pounds. I might make cookies as well. Why don't you also get yourself that fabric you were telling me about? I've sold more lace than I expected and have a bit extra set by."

"Really?" Ellen asked, eyes wide. "You would get that for me?"

"I would. I've the feeling you'll need a new dress soon," her mother said. There was something in her manner that felt strange. Forced, but Ellen didn't want to question her, not if she was going to let her go into town, and possibly see Derek.

"I'll go now," Ellen promised eagerly, leaving the kitchen. She shot a glance at her mother, who was working much slower, and looking lost in thought. There was a sadness about her now, and Ellen wondered if perhaps, once long ago, she and Mrs. Clayton had been friends.

What would that be like? Being friends with someone, only to fall in love and marry someone who then made you become a rival? Ellen wrapped her arms around herself. What a terrible thing. And it might just happen to her and Derek. She swallowed and reached for the basket of lace.

Ellen hurried to town. It was quite quiet today, and after she dropped the lace off and purchased the fabric, she was pleased to see Peter was there at the post office. There wasn't anyone else around either.

She stepped to the counter, and said, "Hello."

"Well, hello," the postmaster told her. "No mail for the Graysons."

"That's all right," Ellen said. "I came here for a different reason."

"Need to post something?" he asked.

"No, that's not it either." Ellen hesitated, then said, "Maggie and the reverend said you might know the answer to a question I have. You see, I'm trying to find out why," she glanced around and lowered her voice, "why my family hates the Claytons so much."

"Ahh." Peter rubbed at his chin. "That's a good question. Why do they think I would know?"

"I guess because your family has been here so long." Ellen asked hopefully, "Do you know anything?"

Peter shook his head. "I'm sorry. I don't. But..." he grew a thoughtful look, "I do have my grandfather's old journals. As postmaster, he kept track of a lot of the town gossip. He was sort of the unofficial newspaper. My grandfather also fancied himself a historian, and wrote down quite a bit about Deepwater."

"Really?" Ellen brightened at that. "I wonder if there's anything in one of them."

"I will look," Peter promised. "To tell the truth, I've always been curious myself. I hate to see a town as small as this with two families against each other. It's not right."

"I agree," Ellen said.

Peter sighed, "Makes me worry too."

"In what way?" Ellen asked.

"Romeo and Juliet. Ever hear of them?" When she shook her head, he told her, "They are characters from one of William Shakespeare's plays. Romeo was from a rival family of Juliet's, but they fell in love."

Ellen felt a jolt in her stomach. "Is...is that so?" she managed.

"That's right. But their families wouldn't have let them be together."

"Did it work out in the end?" Ellen asked. Maybe she could use this story for inspiration to help her with her own situation.

Peter shrugged. "In a way. The families reconciled. But over the deaths of Romeo and Juliet. The two married in secret. And Juliet, in order to avoid marriage to someone else, sought and used a potion that would make it appear as though she had died. Romeo wasn't aware of that, though, and when he found her, poisoned himself to join her."

"Oh no!" Ellen gasped, bringing her hand to her mouth. "What happened when she woke and found out?"

"She killed herself," Peter said solemnly. "By a dagger. So, you see, though it did bring the families together, it was at a terrible loss."

Ellen nodded. It was. And she would not be taking inspiration from that story!

"I promise to tell you if I learn anything," Peter said. "Come back in about a week. That should give me time to read through them. My father had some too."

"Thank you," Ellen told him. "I appreciate it."

"May I ask," Peter said, "why a Grayson wants to find out why they are supposed to hate a Clayton?"

Ellen didn't answer. What was she supposed to say? Her mind spun as she tried to think up something. Would he believe her if she said that she felt it was time to let bygones by bygones?

"I, well, you see," Ellen stammered, and then stopped helplessly. Her eyes found Peter's looking into hers sympathetically.

"I see," he said, and somehow she sensed that he did.

"Please," Ellen whispered. Or maybe she pleaded. She wasn't sure. "Don't tell anyone."

"Let me see what I can learn," he said. "Just...just promise me one thing."

"What's that?" Ellen asked.

"You and Derek won't go to such lengths as Romeo and Juliet."

Someone approached the counter, and Ellen nodded to Peter before she left, stopping for a moment to collect herself at the side of the post office. Taking a deep breath, she headed toward the café to leave a note and search for one.

The story Peter had told her might have ended in a tragedy, but she was praying that hers and Derek's wouldn't.

Chapter 12

Derek forced another bite of oatmeal into his mouth. It tasted like how he imagined glue would. He fought back a cough as the blob gagged him.

"Are you feeling poorly?" his mother asked. "Your color doesn't look right, and you've hardly eaten."

"I'm fine," Derek answered, reaching for the molasses again. A more generous pour might help. He shoved another bite in. His answer wasn't the truth. He didn't feel well, but he also knew the problem.

After Hugh had discovered him and Ellen, Derek had felt sick to his stomach. Though Hugh had promised not to say anything, Derek knew how easily it could happen that something would slip out. And if it did, he didn't care so much about what his parents would say to him. He was worried about what might happen to Ellen.

"Maybe you should rest," his father said. "If you're coming down with something, the rest of us don't need to catch it."

Derek wanted to argue, but he honestly didn't feel well. Staying in bed, lazy as it felt, didn't sound too bad. So, he nodded.

After breakfast, he went to his room. Derek read each of his notes from Ellen and wondered what she was doing right now. Was she helping her parents? Reading? Looking at the heart he'd made her? Maybe she was even writing to him.

But then, that brought up new questions. What should he do? What was the right thing for him? For her?

There was a knock at his door. Hurriedly, he hid her notes to him. With a last glance to be sure nothing incriminating was there, he called, "Come in."

His door opened, and Hugh walked in. "Ma went to town, and Pa's in the barn."

Derek nodded, not sure why his brother was telling him that. But when Hugh crossed his arms over his chest and leaned against the doorframe, Derek's stomach sank, and started hurting even worse. He had the feeling Hugh was going to talk about Ellen.

"You thought about what you're going to do?" Hugh asked.

"About?" Derek said, pretending he didn't know what his brother meant.

"That Grayson girl." Hugh's eyes narrowed. "I promised not to tell, and I won't. But you know I'm right."

"Maybe you are, maybe you aren't," Derek said. "I don't know."

"I'm trying to help you," Hugh said, throwing his hands in the air. "Why are you making this so hard on yourself?"

"Because I want to be happy," Derek answered, just as hotly. "Because I love Ellen. I want to be with her."

"You just think you love her," Hugh retorted. "There are plenty of other women. This town, towns nearby, mail-order brides. You could take out an ad for exactly what you want, and get it. So, why are you fixated on the one person you can't have? Why can't you just do the thing that's best for everyone—including her?"

Derek shook his head. How could he make his brother understand? Sure, he could do those things, any of them. But he didn't want to. "Why haven't you done it?" he asked finally. "Looked for someone else? Gotten just what you want."

His brother didn't answer. Derek shrugged. "Not easy to answer, is it? It's because you don't want anyone else. That's just how I feel. Only, and I hate saying this because I don't want to hurt you, I still have a chance with Ellen. Cara is married, and you might never get to see her again."

Hugh's jaw clenched, and a combination of hurt and anger flashed in his eyes as he nodded. "You're right. She is. But there's something you don't realize."

"What?" Derek asked.

"You don't have a chance with Ellen. No matter what you tell yourself. I'm not saying this because I want you to suffer the way I have. It's because I don't want you to be hurt. I don't want you to have trouble sleeping and trouble eating and trouble just plain living because there's a black cloud over you."

Hugh seemed to realize his voice had gotten louder and lowered it. "You don't think it will happen, but it will when you can't be with her or when her folks or ours find out and one or both of you get in trouble. You know how Pa can be. You really want his temper directed at you? When he'll tell you that you should have known better?"

Derek knew his brother was right. Before he could say anything, Hugh continued. "If you love her, you'll protect her by walking away. It will keep her safe. She can move on. Not know what it's like to feel our parents' anger and disgust toward her. You want her to be treated that way? Or get thrown out and have to figure out how to survive and eat and have a roof over your head? And with a wife to provide for too? Of course not. Tell her goodbye. You know I'm right."

Just then, the front door shut loudly. Derek and Hugh traded looks and headed to the kitchen, where they could hear their father talking to their mother, who was slamming the kettle onto the stove.

"Ma? You okay?" Derek asked.

"I am not," she said, teeth gritted. "I went to the dressmaker because I had spotted the most beautiful fabric the other day. Your father told me to get it as my birthday gift. Do you know what happened?" She didn't even give them a chance to reply before she said, "I was told that Grayson girl bought it. My fabric."

Derek knew it wouldn't be appropriate to suggest she find something else or to say likely Ellen didn't know his mother had her eye on the same fabric. He might not know a lot about women, but he knew enough to know when one had her mind set on something and didn't get it, nothing would be an acceptable substitute.

"Selfish, that's what they are," his father said. "I hope you still got something. Show that girl up."

"I did," his mother sniffed. "Bought two bolts and a shawl. I'd thought about some of the lace I'd seen, but when I heard Marta Grayson made it, I lost interest."

"You don't need that anyway," their father said, putting an arm around her. "Lace is for a woman who needs adornment. You're pretty enough as is. Don't you forget that."

His mother beamed up at him, and Derek left the kitchen quietly and went back to his room. So, Ellen had bought the fabric his mother had wanted. He was sure whenever she wore whatever she made from it, his mother would be full of comments each time she saw her.

Derek sat on the edge of his bed and dropped his head into his hands. This wasn't good. It made things even more difficult. Ellen was wrong. Knowing what caused the original feud wouldn't make things better. There was no fixing anything. Not when each family did things to the other without even meaning to.

There was simply no evening the score or forgiving the other or anything else. He hated to admit it, but Hugh had a point. Maybe it was better to stop things now, before they got worse. Say goodbye. Try to forget about Ellen, push her out of his mind. It didn't mean he had to replace her. Leaving was protecting her.

But he couldn't. He couldn't walk away. Couldn't forget about her. Not when every inch of him loved Ellen. There was always the option to run away. Maybe he should consider it. He was a man now. But the image of Ellen, struggling and work worn if he couldn't provide made him hesitate.

What if they went further west? Got land? Started over. No one would know who they were. It was an idea. But how could he pack and leave and get her there without anyone knowing? Without her reputation being ruined? Reverend Sullivan was sure to refuse marrying them if he knew the plan.

With a groan, he kicked at the foot of his bed. There wasn't an easy answer. Not for anything, it seemed, and especially not their future. What was he going to do?

Chapter 13

For the last week, Ellen's parents had been acting...unusual. There had been whispers, and glances, conversations that stopped when she walked into the room. They hardly let her out of their sight, and as a result, she hadn't been able to visit the café and browse the books or leave a note. She also hadn't been able to follow up with Peter, and see what he'd found out from his grandfather's journals.

However, as much as she longed to know what he'd discovered, she also wanted to know why her parents were acting so strangely, and what it had to do with her. It was obvious it did in some way. Why else would they stop talking when she came into a room?

As they sat in the church pew, Ellen's eyes drifted around the building. There was Peter, sitting next to

Alyssa. Could she get a moment to speak with him? Her eyes darted to her mother. Not likely. She'd asked on the way to town about stopping by the café, but her mother had said no. That she didn't need to borrow another book.

Ellen had felt upset and wanted to protest, but she didn't miss the look her parents had traded. A strong suspicion that they knew something she didn't—or even perhaps knew that she'd been seeing Derek—came over her, and she figured it was better not to argue. Perhaps that was what they'd been whispering about.

Derek. How she missed him. Ellen wondered if he knew that she hadn't left a note not because she hadn't wanted to, but because she hadn't been able to. Her eyes found him sitting next to his brother, his eyes forward, his shoulders tense. His parents looked much the same. Perhaps things had been happening at his home too.

Had his older brother said something to their parents? Had they then told her parents? Ellen worried at the cuff of her dress sleeve and tried not to think such things. Surely, if that were the case, her parents would have come out and said it.

As the church service ended, Ellen's father pulled the reverend aside for a moment. Gabriel's face was hidden from Ellen, but she could still see her father, and he looked serious. They talked, then Gabriel nodded, before reaching out to shake her father's hand. She wished she knew what they were saying. Based on the curious looks around them, she wasn't the only one.

When her father returned, Ellen tried to decipher the look on his stony face, but she wasn't able to, and he didn't offer any explanation. He led them to the church doors and outside. For once, neither of her parents stopped to talk to anyone. Her mother didn't even look up from where she'd been gazing at the ground.

They walked toward their wagon in silence. There was tension in the air. Ellen was acutely aware something was wrong. Her father suddenly said, "Ellen, I've something to tell you."

"What is it, Pa?" Ellen asked. Maybe this was the reason for the strange feeling, and how her parents had been acting for the last week.

Her parents traded looks, and her father drew in a deep breath. "I've decided you are to marry."

Ellen stilled from where she'd been about to climb into their wagon. "What?" She hoped the thundering of her heart wouldn't drown out the words she needed to hear. Why would her father think such a thing? And what did he mean, *he'd* decided? This was the last thing she'd expected to hear.

"That's right. Two towns over, I've a friend who has a son your age. William Stafford. You'll be married here next Sunday." Her father added, "After seeing that Clayton boy and how he was staring at you, and the fact Joe called you a...well, it's the best way to quell any talk."

"I wasn't aware there was any talk," Ellen said, her voice near a whisper. Anger was blossoming within her. Fury. Her hands balled into fists, and she said, "So that's it? No warning? No choice in the groom? You've decided, and that's how it is?"

"Exactly," her father said. "He's a good boy. He'll make you a fine husband. You'll move there, on their farm, after the wedding. But having it here...well, it's a good way to show you aren't for any Clayton."

The words echoed in her mind, and she struggled to grasp them and make sense of what he was saying. "Move?" Ellen was aware her voice was trembling. "What of my friends? All of the things here? You?"

"We'll miss you," her mother said, and Ellen recognized the anguish in her mother's face, "but..."

She didn't finish. She didn't have to. What Ellen's father said was what was going to happen. This was all because she'd spoken to Derek the day they were helping put out the fire at the blacksmith's shop? It made her angry. She closed her eyes for a moment, imagining the horrible experience of getting married to a man she didn't know, when the one she loved was sitting there, watching.

Ellen had never thought her parents cruel, but then again, she'd also never imagined they would force her to do something like this. There was no way around it, unless...

"I won't do it," Ellen said, crossing her arms over her chest. "You can't make me. I'm not going to marry a stranger."

"He's not a stranger," her father said calmly. "I've known his father for a few years. The Staffords are—"

"He's a stranger," Ellen hissed. "And I won't."

"This isn't the place," her mother said, her voice low as she glanced around. "People are starting to stare."

"Let them!" Ellen said. "I won't marry him. And you can't make me."

"Now see here," her father started.

But hot and angry tears filled Ellen's eyes, and she pushed past him wordlessly, past her mother, past the crowd forming, and ran blindly. She didn't know where she was going and, indeed, had no illusions that she'd be able to escape. There was no escape from such a thing, but if she could just get a warning to Derek, let him know she wasn't doing this willingly—

The ground seemed to shake. There was the scream of a horse, and Ellen wiped her eyes on her sleeve just in time to see she'd run out in front of a wagon with two horses, and it was heading straight toward her.

There was no time to move out of the way. She was going to be killed.

Chapter 14

Derek had felt Ellen staring at him the whole of the church service. When they'd first arrived, he'd glanced at her, and though he'd longed to have more than just that incredibly quick glimpse, he knew he couldn't.

It had been a struggle to listen to the sermon. His thoughts were of Ellen. All around the church, other couples sat together. Had any of them experienced such challenges as he and Ellen did? He didn't think so, even if he didn't know their stories too well.

Derek didn't know how much longer he could do this, keep his love for Ellen a secret. Why should they? Why should Ellen try and fix the relationship between their parents? How was any of that their responsibility? He just wanted to love her and be with her.

When the service was over and her father had gone to speak with the reverend, he'd watched, unashamed. In fact, he'd only been disappointed he couldn't hear what was being said.

Gabriel had looked concerned. Hesitant. He had seemed to speak with caution, but in the end had nodded, agreeing to whatever it was Mr. Grayson had been asking about. Derek wished he knew what.

As he joined his family outside, he'd noticed some sort of argument over by the Graysons' wagon. Ellen was upset, her voice was raised, but Derek couldn't make out what she was saying. Her mother was trying to calm her father down, while Ellen looked on in horror, an anguished expression on her face.

"Look at them, making a spectacle of themselves," Derek's mother tsked, coming up next to him.

"Something's wrong," Derek said, before he realized he'd stepped forward.

"Just leave them," his mother sniffed. "Their kind don't appreciate help." She turned away, but Derek didn't. He couldn't. It was as if he knew he had to get closer to Ellen. Find out what was happening.

He watched as she pushed past her parents and rushed toward the street. Derek's legs broke into a run. He wasn't quite sure why. Something was propelling him forward at a speed he hadn't thought himself capable of.

Everything seemed to happen at once. There was a scream, the sound of horses, and then Ellen, standing there, frozen in horror as a wagon barreled toward her.

Derek didn't think twice. He was already there in the road. He threw himself at Ellen. If he could push her out of the way, he might get trampled, but she'd be safe. That was all that was in his mind. As long as she wasn't hurt, he'd spend the rest of his life—however short or painful it was about to be—happy.

He lunged forward, his arms wrapping around her familiar form as he pushed her out of the way. At the last moment, the wagon swerved and sped past them, but not before the side of it clipped him. Pain blossomed through his body, but it didn't matter. Ellen was okay.

With a cry, Ellen scrambled over from where she'd fallen, and flung herself at him. She sobbed into his chest as she clung to him.

People were drawing closer, but Derek didn't care. He wrapped his arms around her, and dropped a gentle kiss on Ellen's head. "My love," he whispered as he held her tightly, "are you hurt?"

"No. Thanks to you," Ellen said, her voice muffled as she spoke into his chest. Then she tensed, and looked up at him, fear on her face. "I have to tell you something."

But before she could say more, her parents were there, pulling Ellen away from him. His parents were next to him

as well, and Derek didn't miss the look of horror on his
mother's face.

"A Clayton," she whispered, as she stared between him
and Ellen. "How could you?"

"How could I what?" Derek asked, suddenly angry.
"How could I have helped her? How could I protect her
from the wagon that nearly hit her? Or how could I fall in
love? Which is it?"

There was a crowd around them, and everyone was
staring at them, but Derek didn't care. He glanced toward
Ellen, but she was gone. Her father had nearly dragged her
across the street and to their wagon. He started toward
them, but his father stopped him.

"We'll talk about this later," he said gruffly. "Don't make
things worse."

Worse. How could they be any worse? Derek simply
nodded, mindful of all the onlookers, and strode toward
their wagon. It was silent on the way home. Derek didn't
miss Hugh's sympathetic looks, nor the confused and hurt
expression of his mother, nor even those of his father,
which were thoughtful, distant.

As soon as the wagon pulled up to the house, his father
said, "Hugh, put the horses up. Derek, into the kitchen.
Sadie, let's eat early."

Everyone nodded, going about their respective locations
or tasks. Derek found himself at the kitchen table, his silent
father across from him and his mother bustling about.

"How'd it happen?" his father finally asked. "I reckon you've been in love for some time. Don't nobody look at a woman like that if he hasn't had time to get to know her."

"I don't know," Derek said quietly. He didn't even look up as his mother set bowls of stew at each place. "We've not seen much of each other. We can't. How could we? She's a Grayson."

"Exactly," his mother said.

"Why can't whatever happened just be part of the past?" Derek asked, looking between his parents. "Why's everything got to be us or them? Even Hugh! He fell in love and couldn't be with her because she was a cousin of a Grayson. How's that fair to him? To her? It's not right."

"It's just how things are," his father said. "Just as well it's out now. You can move on. Forget about her."

"I can't do that," Derek said.

"You have to," his mother said. "Claytons and Graysons don't mix." She hesitated, then said, "But I'm right glad you saved her. She doesn't seem the type to deserve to be hurt that way. Even if she bought my fabric."

"Was noble of you," his father agreed. "Shows us Claytons are the better ones, rushing into danger to help an undeserving Grayson."

"Ma, please," Derek said, sensing she was slightly softer to the idea of him and Ellen than his father was.

His mother hesitated, then said, almost timidly, "Maybe it is time, Joe. Mend our fences. I mean, the boy—"

"It ain't," his father said, and shook his spoon. "Nothing's going to change between our families, just because you were stupid."

Hugh was walking in as Derek stood up so quickly his chair fell backward. "Stupid? Because my heart picked someone you don't like? You don't even know her. I doubt you even know her family well enough to learn what kind of people they are. Maybe they aren't too bad, but we'll never know, will we? It's always got to be us against them."

"Sit down," his father said. "Nothing you can do except get over it."

"I can't," Derek said. "I'm not doing this. Not keeping the hate going forward another generation. Ellen's the one I love. If I don't have your blessing, then I don't care. I don't need it. I only need her."

Derek rushed out of the kitchen, knowing that he likely sounded like a petulant child, unhappy and throwing a tantrum. He didn't care. It was true. He only needed her. As for the rest, finding a way to have her and provide for her, well, he'd just have to figure that out, and quickly.

He had no intention of living in this house any longer. Not when it was abundantly clear, even after today, that there was no chance for him and Ellen.

Chapter 15

"How could you?" Ellen's father snarled as he urged the horses faster. "A Clayton! You were in the arms of a Clayton! You know what kind of history our families have."

"Glen," her mother said quietly, "they are children and have nothing to do with this quarrel."

Any surprise Ellen would have felt at her mother's words was overshadowed instantly by her father's reply.

"And you are my wife, and Ellen my child," her father said. "This just proves I was right to agree to the marriage between her and my friend's son. Now, it's not just to hurt that Clayton boy or protect Ellen, it's to show her what a fool she's been." He turned his steely gaze to her, where she sat, pressed between her parents on the front wagon seat.

"You'll see. Things will turn out fine, and one day you'll understand why we did this."

"I doubt it," Ellen said, refusing to look at him or say more. Anything that she might say would be thrown back at her or make her father angrier. Right now, she could tell he was furious. She stared into her lap, willing the horses to get them home quickly. Hopefully, she'd be allowed the dignity of her room, at least.

"Marta," her father said the moment the wagon pulled up. "Take Ellen to her room and stay there until I'm done."

Done? Ellen wanted to ask what he meant, but didn't dare. There was a wild look in her father's eyes. Crazed. It scared her. Ellen wasn't sure she'd ever seen him look like that. What did it mean? She knew he was about to do something, but what?

Gently, her mother took her arm and led her to her room. The moment she got there, Ellen wrapped her arms around herself as she sat on the edge of the bed.

What should she say? Do? Apologize? She didn't want to apologize for how she'd reacted or even the fact that she loved Derek. Ellen's eyes rose from her lap and found her mother, who had a distant look on her face.

When she realized Ellen was staring at her, her mother quietly said, "Your father has always been against the Claytons. Between us, I realized, seeing you and their son, how perhaps I've let an anger grow within me for a reason

I don't even know, other than that it was a perceived injustice felt by your father."

"And you'll still force me to marry?" Ellen choked out. "Can't you help me, Ma? Please?"

The shutters on her window suddenly slammed closed, and Ellen trembled as a loud thudding started. She knew that sound. She'd heard it once before years ago as a terrible storm swept through Deepwater. Her father was nailing her shutters closed. If they chose to keep her in her room and locked the door, there would be no escape. There would only be darkness, stale air, and the feeling of being a prisoner.

"Your father thinks it best," her mother answered, her voice low and her eyes on her lap.

"But what of you?" Ellen pleaded, throwing herself at her mother's feet. "I've done nothing wrong to be punished in such a way!"

"It's not a punishment," her mother said, taking a hand to stroke Ellen's hair. "It's...it's to protect you."

But Ellen could tell that her mother wasn't sure she believed the words. Ellen knew she didn't. "This is nothing about protecting me," she said, her voice low. "It's about hurting a Clayton. Derek doesn't deserve that. He's done nothing but treat me kindly. You saw, today he saved me. That wasn't the first time."

Ellen wondered if it would make a difference to tell her mother how he'd saved her from the rattlesnake. She wasn't sure it would matter. Regardless, she knew one thing. Sitting back on her heels, Ellen shook her head. "I'll have no part in this feud moving forward. None. The Grayson hurt and anger over whatever happened ends with me."

Her mother didn't answer, but Ellen didn't miss the tear that slipped down her face as she rose and walked to the bedroom door. Heavy footsteps on the stairs sounded, and Ellen's father appeared.

"Marta, why don't you see to dinner?" he suggested. Then he added, "Ellen, you'll stay here until the wedding. The only way you're getting out of this room is if I feel you aren't going to try and run off."

"Where would I go?" Ellen asked quietly. She tried hard to keep her voice level, to not show hurt or anger or anything that might be considered rebellion and make things worse. "There is nowhere. You've made it abundantly clear I have no choice but to do what you say."

Her father didn't answer, but the heavy oak door closed behind him, and Ellen heard the click as the lock slid into place. She walked to the window and pushed, lightly at first and then harder against the shutters. The wood wouldn't budge. There was hardly a crack where the boards fit together.

With a shuddering breath, Ellen began to walk slowly around her room in a circle. The walls seemed to close in around her and the air felt heavy. It was hard to breathe. A surge of anxiety grew in Ellen until it nearly overwhelmed her. She was trapped. There was nothing she could do. Worst of all, in exactly one week, she'd belong to another man, be in another's arms.

No, that wasn't right. She might be married, but the man would never have her heart. That belonged to Derek.

Ellen's hand went to the small pocket in her dress, and she curled her fingers around the heart Derek had made her. Was today's embrace and this small piece of him all she was to ever have of Derek? If so, she prayed her memory never faded. If only there was a way to tell him what was happening. She'd never had a chance to. What would he think when he saw her, married before the congregation next Sunday?

Would Derek think this was of her choosing? Would he even stay? Or, maybe he was also being punished by his parents, and would have no idea until it was too late.

Ellen's shaking legs gave out and she collapsed to the floor, her head on her arms as she sobbed. She wished there was a way out of this. But that was the problem, wasn't it? She could wish all she wanted, but none of it would come true.

She was trapped, and being forced into this against her will. And nothing could change or stop it.

Chapter 16

"What do you think?"

Derek startled. He'd forgotten where he was and had let himself get lost in worry over Ellen. Quickly, he ran his hands down the new shirt Josiah had sewn in his tailor shop. "This might be the best fitting shirt I've ever had," he said. With a small shake of his head, he added, "Not even my mother can do stitches this fine, and she's quite a seamstress."

The tailor laughed. "It's practice. A good deal of practice. So, since this one is to your liking, take it with you, and I'll have the other two ready in a week."

"That sounds good," Derek said, picking up his old shirt and folding it to carry home. He knew it was futile, especially after the way Ellen's parents had dragged her home a few days ago, but he planned to go to the cafe just the same, and see if there was any word from her.

"I missed seeing your rescue Sunday," Josiah said, as he scribbled on a small notepad. "But I bet your parents are very proud of you, and Ellen's parents grateful."

"Uh, I suppose," Derek said, though it couldn't have been further from the truth.

"You don't think?" Josiah asked.

That's right. The tailor hadn't been living in Deepwater long. Derek sighed, and ran a hand through his hair. "No, I don't. I think it made things worse between our families. I've no idea why, but for generations, they've been against each other. I guess it was expected to continue between me and Ellen. But that's not exactly what happened."

"I see." Josiah set down his pencil and pushed his glasses a little higher on his nose. "That does make things complicated."

"It does," Derek agreed. "I'm worried now her father will do something and I'll never see her again."

Josiah was quiet for a moment. Derek hadn't expected the man to have an answer to his problems, so he was surprised when the tailor suddenly said, "Do you want that?"

"What? Of course not!" Derek said. "I love Ellen."

"Does she know?" Josiah asked.

"She does. I'm sure of that."

Josiah crossed his arms against his chest. "I almost lost Ginny, not just because I was struggling with the demons of my past, but also because I wasn't clear enough on how I felt about her. I'm fortunate things worked out the way they did for us, but they could have ended up with both of us hurt and lonely."

"That's how it's going to be here," Derek said. "There's no help for it."

"What's stopping you from being together?" Josiah asked.

"Our parents," Derek said.

Josiah opened his mouth, then closed it. Derek furrowed his brow. "What are you thinking but not saying?"

"I think there's nothing wrong with being respectful to your parents," Josiah said slowly, "but a time comes a man's got to do what's best by him. Especially when it comes to being with the woman he loves. Not," he added hastily, "that I'm insinuating anything or trying to get into your business. I'm just speaking from experience.

"My first wife was forced into our marriage. I didn't find that out until later, and I've always wondered if she's happy now. She wasn't then. Neither was I. After meeting Ginny and feeling real love," a silly grin formed on the tailor's face, and Derek knew it was the same one that he got thinking about Ellen, "I wouldn't want anyone to not experience such a wondrous thing."

Derek nodded slowly. "You've given me a lot to think on," he said. "While I would hope Ellen's folks never forced her into marrying someone, or my folks me, you are right that if that happened, neither of us would deserve that. I know arranged marriages can work out. But just as many don't. Now that I've had this happiness, I don't want to let go of it."

"I can't tell you what to do," Josiah said kindly, "but I'm always here if you need a friend."

"I appreciate it," Derek said. He moved toward the door and stopped. "Thank you."

He pushed open the door and walked out. All around Deepwater, there was activity. People walking to this place or that, the weekly stage loading with its passengers who'd just barreled out of the cafe in a hurry from their meal, a line snaking around the post office as the townsfolk waited eagerly to see if they had any letters.

Yet, Derek felt alone. Like he was just watching, not really a part of anything. He knew there was no point, but he walked to the cafe. Carissa and Maggie were clearing away the tables cluttered with dirty dishes.

"Here for a bite?" Maggie asked as he approached.

"A muffin and a book," Derek said.

"Cider?" Carissa asked, already pulling a muffin out of the display case.

"Yeah, sure," Derek said. He hadn't wanted to eat there, but he also didn't want to appear rude.

He made his way to the books, checking each. There was nothing from Ellen. Derek swallowed hard as he made his way to where Carissa had set his food. He shouldn't have expected there to be, but still, there was a keen loss.

The cafe door opened, but Derek didn't look up from the book he was pretending to read until someone sat across from him.

"Reverend," Derek greeted him.

"Gabriel," the man corrected. "I feel so old when people call me Reverend."

Derek chuckled, but nodded. "What can I do for you?" he asked, though secretly he hoped that the man would leave him be. After his conversation with Josiah, he wasn't in the mood for more.

But the reverend didn't answer. And, perhaps, for the first time since he'd met the man, Gabriel seemed hesitant. Usually one to talk, even when it wasn't welcome, today he looked as though he wasn't sure what to say.

"You're making me nervous," Derek admitted.

"I find myself in a terrible position," Gabriel said quietly. "Something is going to happen that I don't feel is right. Yet, I am bound by confidentiality." He studied Derek carefully.

"And you think I can help?" Derek asked.

"I don't know. I also don't know if it would make things worse." Gabriel sighed. "How is Ellen? After you saved her from the wagon? I've not passed any of her family in town."

"I have not seen her," Derek said. "I wish I knew. She did seem okay though, afterward."

Before her father dragged her away. But he wasn't going to add that part.

Gabriel nodded slowly. "That's good. Do you ever...check on her? Visit her home?"

"Of course not," Derek said, in surprise. "You know how our families are."

"Right, right. I don't even know why I asked." Gabriel stood. "Maybe you should. That's all."

The reverend walked out, looking...miserable. Derek stared after him, and when he stood himself, noticed Maggie watching the departing reverend with a frown.

"Never seen him act like that," she said.

"Me either." Derek said, "He seems out of sorts. Why, he even suggested I visit Ellen. But I can't. You know that. He does too. I wonder why he'd say such a thing. Something doesn't seem right with him."

Maggie shrugged. "No idea. But when a man of God says something, you ought to listen."

There was a clatter from the kitchen, and Maggie turned to the kitchen door and hurried in. Derek left with a sigh. What was wrong with the two of them? He couldn't go over there. Couldn't see Ellen, no matter how much he wanted to. It would make things worse.

Though, as he walked home, a book and his old shirt tucked under his arm, a small voice kept asking him just how much worse it could get.

Chapter 17

She had to get word to Derek. That was the sole thought in Ellen's mind. For the last few days she'd been shut in her room, Ellen had spent a lot of time thinking. After all, there wasn't anything else to do.

Last night, it had come to her, just what she'd do. She was going to run away. Before the wedding or after, she wasn't sure, but Ellen knew that was the only way she could escape and have a chance at happiness. Of course, she needed to do it before her wedding vows if she was to have any hope of ever being with Derek.

And that meant seeing him.

She was sure she could find her way to his home, but would that cause trouble for her? It might. The best thing to do would be to ask someone to pass along a message for her. She had one written, and folded into a tiny square. Now, she just had to be around someone to pass it to.

The key sounded in her lock, and Ellen composed herself, making sure no expression that might betray her was on her face. Her mother walked in, holding a tray.

"I thought you might be hungry," she said, as her gaze fell on the hardly touched plate from this morning.

"I find I have little appetite," Ellen said quietly.

Her mother nodded. She glanced over her shoulder then, and came closer to Ellen. "I know this hasn't been easy for you," she said. "Perhaps tell your father you agree. He'll let you out of your room."

That was something Ellen had thought about as well. But she wasn't sure her father would believe her. To be sure, she wouldn't have the same freedom as before. It might even be worse. Instead of being alone, in her room, she'd be with one of her parents, constantly under their watchful eye.

"You know it's not right," Ellen answered. "Why should I agree? Would you have?" Before her mother could answer, she said, "Of course not. But you were never in this position. Your parents let you marry the man you loved."

"Ellen," her mother said, her voice so soft she could hardly hear it. "I'm trying to—"

Her mother stopped and stepped back hastily, grabbing up the breakfast tray. "I'll be back in a while with some tea," she said, as though nothing more had been said.

Then she turned, moving away just as Ellen's father appeared in the doorway.

"Ready to see reason?" he asked.

"Are you?" Ellen answered.

The door closing and locking again was her only answer. She'd not expected anything else.

It was two days before Sunday. She was almost out of time. Her mother had encouraged her to use the new fabric she'd loved so much for a wedding dress, but Ellen refused. She'd wear the most somber thing she owned. That fabric would never be used for a new dress unless she had a happy occasion, and her marriage to a stranger was not such a thing.

It grew late in the day. Her mother brought tea and left. Ellen would have ignored it but for her thirst. She picked up the cup and drank deeply, then poured more from the small pot. Her mother had made her favorite cookies, but it was no good. She wasn't hungry.

But as Ellen bumped the plate, she saw a small slip of paper underneath. Curious, she picked it up to see what was written on it.

Take heart.

What did that mean? What in this situation was there to take heart in? She thought back to earlier, when her mother seemed as though she were trying to say something. But Ellen couldn't get her hopes up that her mother was trying to help her. No, if anything was to be done, she'd have to figure out a way to do it herself.

Ellen studied the slip of paper, and then folded it, putting it in her pocket next to the small heart from Derek. She curled up on her bed, feeling an odd mix of exhaustion and restlessness.

Past her door, she could hear footsteps. They sounded like her mother's. Was it mealtime already? The key turned in the lock, but Ellen didn't want to move.

"Are you awake?" her mother asked. "I've something to tell you."

Ellen couldn't bear whatever bad news might be given to her, but she also didn't blame her mother—as much—for her role in this. With a sigh, she sat up. "No. I can't sleep."

"The wedding has been postponed by a day," her mother said. "You'll be married Monday."

"What difference does a day make?" Ellen asked.

Her mother drew close, and took her hands into hers. "It could make a great deal. I wish I could do more, my darling girl."

Before Ellen could say anything, her mother had released her grasp with a choked sob and left.

Ellen stared at the door, and then slowly sank down on the floor of her room. She wrapped her arms around her knees, and rested her head overtop. She must have eventually fallen asleep, for the next thing Ellen knew her father was at her door, telling her to hurry and dress for Sunday services.

It felt as though her arms and legs were entirely too heavy. Ellen put on her second-best Sunday dress, a pale blue one with small flowers on it, and buttoned up her boots. As her father walked with her down the stairs, Ellen tried not to stare. How different it felt being out of her room.

Her eyes feasted on the things she'd once taken for granted. The piano in the corner of the room, the worn chair her mother loved to sit in and knit or read. The small collection of books.

"Hurry now," her father said gruffly.

Ellen obeyed, and went to the wagon, sitting next to her mother on the bench seat. The ride to church was quiet. It was a relief to be inside of the church building, listening to Dirk play the opening hymn. Samantha led them in song, and Ellen felt goosebumps break out as they all sang.

But it was all over far too soon. Ellen looked around frantically, hoping to see Derek, but she couldn't find him. None of her friends were nearby either. Her one and only chance to pass along a message, and it was hopeless.

Just as her father started to lead them away, the reverend approached. "Mr. Grayson," he said. "May I have a word?"

Her father nodded and walked away with Gabriel. At the same time, his lovely wife Laura and Samantha approached.

"I need to speak with someone," her mother said quietly. "Can I trust you to walk to the wagon?"

"I'll be sure of it," Laura said, linking her arm through Ellen's. "I was hoping to have a moment with Ellen."

Her mother nodded, looking distracted. Ellen allowed herself to be led outside. Once there, she found Samantha at her other elbow.

"My dear girl," Laura said, concern in her eyes. "You don't look well."

"I'm not," Ellen said, fighting back a sob. "Please! Please help me! Can you get a message to Derek Clayton?"

"What kind of a message?" Samantha asked.

Her voice trembling, and her mind knowing she might not have much time at all, Ellen quickly told Laura and Samantha everything. From the moment she'd fallen in love with Derek, and how he'd rescued her from the snake, to how they'd been writing notes, and meeting, to how she'd been locked in her room and was being forced to marry someone she'd never met.

"Oh, my dear," Samantha cried, wrapping her arms around her. "How much you must ache!"

"If I am never to see Derek again, so be it," Ellen said through her tears, "but I can't bear the thought of him thinking I didn't care. Please! Please tell him this is not of my choosing. I'm going to run away. Tomorrow, on the way here. I don't know if I'll make it, but I'm going to try and get on Clayton land."

"My friend," Laura said, taking one of her hands and squeezing it. "Is that really the best thing to do?"

"There's nothing else to do!" Ellen said.

Samantha offered her a handkerchief, and gently said, "You can't run from your problems. I would know."

"What am I to do then?" Ellen asked.

"Find the courage within you to do what needs to be done," Samantha said.

"But what is that?" Ellen asked, looking between the two women.

Laura whispered, "What does your heart tell you?"

As though she could find the answer by looking around, Ellen's eyes swept over the church grounds. Her father and the reverend were talking, but looked as though they were nearly finished. Her mother was in the garden, talking to another woman who...who looked a great deal like Mrs. Clayton, but she couldn't be sure. Just then, she saw Derek's older brother approach them, almost hesitantly.

What was going on?

Ellen turned to Laura to ask if she knew what was going on, but she saw her father shaking Gabriel's hand, as though they were done talking. Her mother must have seen, and was walking quickly toward her.

The moment she got there, Laura and Samantha vanished, as though they'd never been there. Ellen searched her mother's face. Her mother's eyes were red, likely matching her own, and she seemed...different.

There was no time to ask, though. Ellen climbed into the wagon, and offered her mother her hand to help her before their father arrived.

"Take heart," her mother whispered, and then nothing more was said.

Chapter 18

Hugh stood in the kitchen doorway, watching as Derek ate. "Ma told me to tell you something."

"Don't want to hear it," Derek said.

"You'll want to," Hugh said quietly. "Wish you'd come with us today."

"You know I couldn't." Derek glared at his brother. "Pa sent me out yesterday for those lost cattle and I didn't get back until just now."

"I know. I didn't mean—never mind. I don't know how to say this. So I'm just going to say it."

"What?" Derek asked.

"Ellen's getting married."

Derek's mouth felt as dry as dust. Married. Before he could say anything, Hugh hurriedly kept talking. "Not willingly."

That helped, but not by much. Derek's heart still ached. He'd never see her again. Never hold her. Never get to kiss her. He closed his eyes. "I almost wish you hadn't told me."

"But you aren't going to believe what happened." Hugh shook his head. "I can't believe it myself."

"Guess I never will, if you don't tell me," Derek said, though his words felt dull to his ears. Slow. It felt a struggle to talk. "But if you're here to gloat, I don't want to hear it. You've just told me I've lost the woman I love."

"Not yet, you ain't," Hugh said.

Derek's jaw clenched. He stood from the table and shook his head. "Hurry up then. I want to be by myself, and I can't do that until you go away."

His mother walked in just then. "Hugh. Keep your father in the barn as long as you can," she said, just as calmly as if they were discussing what she was making for dinner.

Derek shot her a confused look, but Hugh nodded. The moment he was gone, his mother faced him.

"Marta Grayson came up to me at church," she said. A strange look came over her face, and for a moment, Derek wondered if she was about to cry.

His mother took in a deep breath, and said, "She told me Ellen's father is forcing her to marry someone a few towns over. They were supposed to marry today, but it's been delayed until tomorrow."

"I hope they'll be happy," Derek said through his gritted teeth.

Bad enough he'd had to hear it from Hugh. Now his mother? He was sure his father would be smirking when he walked in.

"Listen to me, boy," his mother said, her tone sharp.

Derek's eyes shot to hers. She never spoke like that. "Ma?"

"Who knows how long we have. She doesn't know him. Doesn't love him. But I know, if there was anyone in this world who would love my son the way he deserves to be loved, it's her." His mother stood taller somehow, though her eyes darted toward the kitchen window, and the barn.

Derek stared at her, not sure he was hearing what he thought she was saying.

"Now, it's too late for me to help Hugh, and I'll spend my life regretting that," his mother said, "but Marta was able to convince Glen to delay the wedding by one day. It's tomorrow. So you have time to stop it."

"Stop it? Ma, are you..." Derek shook his head. "But...."

Words weren't coming. He wasn't even sure what he was trying to say. Or think. His mind was numb right now.

"Marta agrees with me. It's gone on long enough. She and I have come to an understanding, and if our husbands want to continue to argue, that's their decision. She wants a man for her daughter who loves her. And she saw that in you." His mother looked at him. "Do you understand what I'm telling you? What I'm trying to do? The two of you...it can stop. It can end."

Derek nodded wordlessly. "But Pa..."

"He'll be furious. So I don't know what to tell you. Try to fix things or try to run. The choice is yours. You need to go to the Grayson house now. Marta is trying to distract Glen. This is all we can do for the two of you. A short head start. Do you understand?"

His mother's voice was strained, high-pitched. Tears were pouring down her cheeks.

"Ma," Derek said, pulling her into his arms and hugging her as if it would be the last time he ever did. It very well might.

"Go, my boy," she whispered. "And know that I love you, and I know Ellen does too. You have my blessing, if none other."

Derek nodded, unable to speak around the lump in his throat, and then turned, running. He didn't get far, as his father came toward him, Hugh rushing behind him with panic on his face.

"You aren't going anywhere," his father said. "Get back in the house." His eyes sought Derek's mother. "What have you done? Agreeing to such a thing."

"I won't," Derek said. "It's nothing Ma did. But I'm going after Ellen."

"Not and being my son, you ain't," his father growled. "We don't mix our kind."

"What is our kind?" Derek asked, raising his voice. He saw Hugh backing away, heading to the barn, not that he blamed him for running, and turned his attention back to his father. "Can't you see how this goes? Generation after generation, the hate and the anger, and why? You don't know! Ma doesn't know! I bet they don't either. But you do it because it's habit. Didn't you ever stop to think the effect it's had on everyone? On Hugh? On me? On Ma?

"Mrs. Grayson was her best friend. She gave her up because of the feud. Gave her up for you. Can't we stop? Can't we make things better?" Derek shook his head. "We can't, though, can we? Someone wants blood. Is that what it will take to stop this? Blood? I'll give them mine then," Derek shouted.

Hugh suddenly appeared just behind his father. His brother hadn't run off. He had saddled Derek's horse and had it at the ready, a fierce look on his face as he started to jog, forcing the mare to a slow run and heading right toward Derek.

Derek pushed past his father, jumping on the mare and racing as though his life depended on it. Maybe it did. He wasn't sure.

Derek hoped Hugh knew how grateful he was to him, and his mother, for her part. He prayed one day he could tell them so. He didn't think his father would understand, but he knew he'd come after them, and his only thought now, instead of trying to run away with Ellen, was to warn her family.

It might be the last thing he'd ever do, but he'd do it because he loved her and it was time for this to end. He'd warn them and stand his ground. God would have to do the rest.

Derek had no regrets other than one. He wished he'd had more time with Ellen. He'd meant every word he said. If blood would end this war between their families, he'd give his willingly. Anything to keep Ellen from being forced into marriage.

Chapter 19

"She'll be married and gone tomorrow," Ellen could hear her mother saying. "Let me spend the rest of the day with her, here, in our home. Please, Glen. I might never see her again."

Ellen couldn't hear her father's reply through the door, but seconds later, the lock sounded, and her door opened. Ellen's mother stepped in, and her eyes were red, as though she'd been crying. The sight made Ellen's chest squeeze with guilt.

It was almost as bad as the guilt she'd been feeling about Derek rushing after her and knocking her away from the oncoming wagon. He had put himself in grave danger. In fact, had things not gone as they had, it was possible Derek could have been severely injured, or even died.

She was so tired of feeling guilt. Guilt over loving Derek, over meeting with him, over hurting her parents. Ellen felt an overwhelming sadness as she looked at her mother. Still, she had no choice. She had to ask.

"Ma?" she said softly. "Can I...can I ask a favor of you? Before..."

She couldn't say it. The words would come out hurtful and bitter, if she lied and said if she married that stranger. But if she told the truth, that she was tempted to run and hide, that she hoped to seek out Derek, that might just serve to get her locked up or in worse trouble.

"If I can do it, I will," her mother promised. She sat next to Ellen on the edge of her bed. "I know that things are not going as you'd hoped."

"I don't want to talk about it," Ellen said, wiping her eyes. "It makes it worse." She took a deep breath and said, "I guess you know now. That...that Derek and I..."

Her mother nodded. To Ellen's surprise, she didn't look judgmental, but sympathetic. Maybe she could ask her question.

"Would you please just deliver a note to him? Or his parents? So that I can say goodbye? And he'll know what's happened to me?"

Her mother nodded, and took the envelope Ellen handed her. Ellen knew that it likely would be opened, that it might be read by her parents or his. That it may not even reach Derek. But she had to try, and assure him of her love, even if she couldn't tell him that she was running away.

Hopefully, the message about meeting the place he first saved her would be enough. She knew she couldn't wait there long, or she'd be found, but she could try.

Ellen's mother said, "Why don't you come downstairs?"

"Shouldn't I pack?" Ellen asked dully. She glanced around her room. A large trunk had been brought in for her, but she hadn't filled it. In fact, she hadn't put anything in it.

In part, it was because Ellen had hoped this was all just a dream, that she wasn't getting married to a stranger. The rest was, by not packing, it was a form of protest. She didn't want this, and she didn't plan to make it easy at all for them.

Her mother didn't answer. Instead, she bit her lip and twisted her fingers. Ellen wondered what that meant. Why her mother was acting so strangely. She seemed like she wanted to say something, and Ellen did want to ask her why she'd been talking to Mrs. Clayton, and what she'd meant by *take heart*, but she worried her father was nearby. She knew he'd be quite unhappy if he learned such things.

Ellen wondered at the change that had seemed to come over her mother, and wished that her father would soften, the way it seemed her mother might be.

Just then, there was a knock at the front door. Both she and her mother turned toward the sound. Ellen followed her mother down the stairs. She wasn't sure where her father was, but he must not have noticed whoever was visiting.

As her mother opened the door, Ellen stood slightly back, and then gasped. It was Derek!

"Ellen, I love you," he burst out, stepping forward to grab her hands. "I want you to know that. I heard you were getting married. I hope I'm not too late. I don't know how long we have. My pa, he's angry and on his way because he knows I'm here. I've come to warn you, but I'm not going to let him hurt you." His eyes went to her mother. "Or you, ma'am."

Somehow, Ellen had moved forward, and she was outside now, close to him. Every part of her longed to step into his arms, to seek comfort, but she wasn't sure if she should, with her mother there. Derek pleaded, "Maybe we can fix things if we aren't here. Come with me. We'll run away if we have to. Be my wife. There's no one else I will love for the rest of my life."

Ellen's heart felt as though it might burst, it was pounding so hard. She had no idea what to say. She longed to say yes, but her mother was there, watching. Did her reaction matter? It did...and Ellen wanted her blessing. But then she realized something.

Watching. Her mother was watching. Not saying anything.

"I love you, Derek," she said, falling into his arms and relaxing once they were around her, and hoping that meant her mother accepted it. "I'm so glad to see you."

"Your parents are coming," Ellen's mother said. Then she whispered, "And my husband."

"I'll give up my family if it will make your father content," Derek said, releasing his embrace but still holding one of Ellen's hands. "Anything that will get him to agree to let you marry me. And I mean it." His jaw clenched, and he said, "Or else I'll make my own way, and provide for you. I promise. The choice is yours. We can leave now or we can stay and fight for us."

"I know you will," Ellen said, feeling both proud of the man before her and terrified at the choice she must make. Which would be better?

"Get away from my daughter!" her father shouted, as he got closer. He was about a dozen paces away and closing in quickly.

"Glen," her mother said, stepping between them.

"Marta! What are you doing?" he asked in shock, as he peered over her shoulder at Ellen and Derek.

"Something I ought to have done a long time ago," Ellen's mother said, though she could see her trembling.

The Clayton wagon rolled to a stop just then, and Derek's parents clamored down. As Mr. Clayton headed toward her, Ellen's jaw dropped as Mrs. Clayton broke into a run, her skirts held up to her calves, and stood next to her mother, making a wall and keeping their fathers at a distance.

"Joe, enough," Mrs. Clayton said as she held out a hand. "Marta and I have decided this is foolish. They have no argument with each other. We shouldn't either. In fact," she turned to Ellen's mother, "I never had a quarrel with you, Marta. I've missed you."

"I've missed you too, Sadie," Ellen's mother sniffled. "Can you ever forgive me for the times I tried to get under your skin?"

"Only if you'll forgive me," Mrs. Clayton said, near tears herself. "We will hug properly later." She stood as tall as her small frame would allow, and fixed her sharp gaze on her husband. "You can give our children your blessing and bring our families together or you can go through us much smaller women while we do our best to give them a running start."

Ellen was sure her jaw had been open the whole time because it was starting to ache. Where had this come from? Their mothers, uniting both to help them and to become friends again and put a stop to whatever had caused this wasn't something she'd ever imagined. She glanced at Derek, who also looked in shock.

"Now see here!" Mr. Clayton nearly choked on his words, his face was so red.

"Have you women lost your minds?" Ellen's father yelled.

"Don't you talk to my wife that way," Mr. Clayton said, shoving Ellen's father.

"You get off my property, Clayton, before I get my rifle," her father shouted, pushing back.

Ellen felt Derek tugging her backward slightly. Before her, their mothers were backing up as well. Perhaps a little in fear, but also to give them more space. Ellen wasn't sure which, but she knew she'd never forget this day, and the incredible love and sacrifice the two women before her were showing.

"Try it!" Mr. Clayton said. "I've got mine too." He shoved her father again, just as another wagon rode into the yard and a familiar face stared, first in shock and then disapprovingly.

Everyone stopped, freezing to the spot as Reverend Gabriel Sullivan jumped down from the wagon, striding closer, and fixed each with a look. Calmly, he said, "No one is shooting anyone. Not while I'm here and not when I'm gone. Now, might I inquire as to what's got everyone so upset?"

"It's his fault!" Ellen's father said, pointing his finger, at the exact moment Derek's father did.

Ellen shot a look at Derek. Was now the time to run? Or the time to put the past behind them once and for all?

Chapter 20

Derek wasn't sure if he should use the reverend as a distraction and get Ellen away from their angry fathers, or if he should try to make things better. A quick glance at Ellen showed she was as shocked as everyone else there, as the reverend drew closer.

"I wasn't expecting to ride up and see a shoving match," Gabriel said as he glanced among everyone there. "Can we sit down and talk about what's got everyone so upset? Apologize and mend fences?"

"There's no mending anything," Derek's father growled. "Not when a Grayson is involved."

"That goes double, when there's a Clayton stirring up things," Ellen's father snapped in reply.

"Does anyone even know what the problem is?" Ellen asked. Derek's eyes landed on her, just like everyone else's did. Before he could say anything, she continued, "Because I don't think anyone does. I don't think the Claytons know why they hate the Graysons. I'm also not sure the Graysons know why they hate the Claytons."

"It's always been that way," Derek's father said.

"But, what if it wasn't?" Derek asked. He glanced between his parents. "What if we all got along? Or, used to get along?"

"You're just saying that because this Grayson girl has you tricked," his father said. Then he turned toward Derek's mother. "And for some reason, you have been as well! I don't know what's gotten into you, Sadie! I thought you were on my side!"

"I thought the same, Marta," Ellen's father said, as he crossed his arms and glared at his wife.

"The only side I'm on," Ellen's mother said, "is that of practicality. Ellen's right. I don't know why we don't like the Claytons. I don't know why his parents didn't." She hesitated, looked at Derek's mother, and softly said, "I just know it's gotten in the way of friendship, and in the case of our children, something more."

"That's right," Derek's mother said. "And we're tired of seeing how much hurt we can dole out to the other. It's time to stop. Please. Don't let this go on another generation. Someone has to put a stop to this, and Marta and I plan to. For our sakes, for our children's sakes, and for your sakes."

"What does your fool decision have to do with me?" Ellen's father asked.

"Glen," Ellen's mother scolded. "Sadie's right, and you know it."

"Maybe we can get to the bottom of this," Gabriel said. "Can we sit somewhere? Talk? Perhaps someone will know something and we can figure out how this all started, and also figure out how to move forward, for all those involved."

Everyone glanced at the other, but nodded.

"Glen, will you get a few chairs from the kitchen?" Ellen's mother asked. "I've got water in the kettle. Let me make something for us to drink. Ellen, will you help?"

"Yes, Ma," Ellen said, starting toward her mother.

Derek didn't want her to leave, worried this might be a trick of some sort, but his mother seemed to know that, and offered, "Can I help somehow?"

"That would be wonderful," Ellen's mother said.

The women went into the house, and Glen appeared a moment later carrying two chairs that he set on the porch. There were already two rocking chairs and a wide bench there, along with another chair. Derek hoped he'd be allowed to sit next to Ellen on the bench.

It wasn't too long before the women returned. His mother was holding a platter of cookies and sliced bread with jam. Ellen had a tray with cups, and her mother a tray with a jug of water and a teakettle.

"Thank you, ladies," Gabriel said. "This looks wonderful."

Derek sat on the bench and tried not to grin when Ellen sat near him. This was a serious moment—it was also a monumental one. While both sets of parents looked uncomfortable, Derek hoped that they wouldn't get upset again.

As much as he longed to, he didn't take Ellen's hand. That might cause problems, and since things were calming down, he didn't want to add fuel to the fire. Or the feud. Luckily, the platter of sugar cookies was a good diversion.

"Does anyone want to explain what I drove up to?" Gabriel asked. His tone was curious, and he didn't have an ounce of judgment in it. He never would, Derek thought, not with his previous background. The man understood people, and he was firsthand acquainted with hardships and hurt, and that made him more than a man of God. It made him someone who was a true friend if needed.

"It's my fault," Derek said. "I knew Ellen's parents wouldn't want me near her. But I couldn't help it. I fell in love with her, and couldn't stay away."

Ellen's cheeks pinked, and she shyly put her hand on his arm, squeezing gently before removing it. "It was my fault as well. I love Derek, and I wanted to see him. I was upset that Pa didn't want me around him, and wanted me to marry someone else. Someone I didn't know."

Gabriel nodded. "I warned him that might not be a good idea."

Ellen's father sighed, looking down at his boots. "You did."

"I wish you'd have listened," Ellen's mother said softly. "Though I know why you did it."

Ellen's father nodded. "Doesn't change things. I...I reckon I was too proud to listen. To any of you. I should have known when Derek risked his life to save her from that wagon what they had was real."

Ellen turned to Derek, anguish on her face. "I feel terrible that I put you in such a position. And, I'm so sorry, Mr. and Mrs. Clayton. I wasn't thinking, and I didn't know Derek was nearby or would do that. It wasn't until later that I realized just how hurt he could have been."

"Our boy's always been brave, and thinking of others," Derek's father said, as he put an arm around Derek's mother's shoulders. "I suspect even if you'd told him not to, he'd have done it anyway."

"That's right, I would have," Derek said. "I'd rather be hurt and suffer, if it meant that you were safe."

Ellen's father cleared his throat. "I owe you a debt of gratitude," he said. "I'm sorry to have gotten angry. Sometimes a man does that when he doesn't know how else to act."

"There's no need to apologize to me, sir," Derek said. "But," he glanced at his parents, "if you really mean that, a debt, I'd like to ask that you pay it by putting whatever this is between our families in the past. Let us move forward, together. United."

Gabriel nodded, and said, "I have only been here in Deepwater for a few years, but I do know that this was going on before I came."

"Marta and I used to be friends," Derek's mother said. "Even after she got married. It...it wasn't until Joe and I started courting that things changed. I hated to do it, but Joe warned me I couldn't be friends with her anymore if I wanted to marry him. I hated to lose my dear friend," his mother continued, "but at the time, I was so love-struck, I thought that he was fooling."

"I remember how hurt I was," Ellen's mother said. "I understood though. Glen wasn't happy about you marrying him. Yet," she grew a thoughtful look, "I don't ever recall why. Just...just that he didn't like Joe."

Ellen's father shifted in his chair. "Well, my pa didn't like the Claytons. Grandpa either. I guess I just let their opinions form my own."

"This has been going on for some time now," Gabriel said. "I'm proud of you for considering putting it in the past."

Derek's father said, "It was the same at our place. I don't rightly know why, but nobody on my side ever liked the Graysons." He hesitated, and gave a small shrug. "I suppose it never occurred to me to find out why." He gave Derek a wry grin. "Seems my son is smarter than me."

Derek shook his head, "No, not me. It's Ellen. She's been determined to find out why and bring us all together."

Ellen laughed lightly. "If I'd known nearly getting run over by a wagon was all it took, I'd have done it sooner."

Everyone joined in the laughter, and Derek sighed. He reached for Ellen's hand, and with none of their parents protesting, held it gently. "I'm glad that we are here, now, trying to rebuild what was lost," he said. "I just wish I knew why everybody hated everybody."

"I know the answer to that," a new voice said, and Derek turned to see Peter standing there, a book in hand.

Chapter 21

Ellen stood in surprise as the postmaster approached, a hesitant expression on his face. "I was coming to see you, Ellen," he said, "because of the question you'd asked. Seems like my timing is good. Everyone's here."

"It is," she said eagerly. "I can't wait to hear what you've learned. But first, let me get another cup."

In short order, Ellen's father had brought out another chair, her mother had refilled the cookie platter, and Ellen had brought out more tea and water.

After Peter had taken a few sips, he set his cup down gently, and said, "So, it seems the Graysons and Claytons are wanting to set aside differences?"

There was some hesitation as her father glanced at Mr. Clayton, but both nodded, and Ellen felt a little of the tightness within her ease.

"I'm glad to hear it," Peter said. "Because what I've learned is...something else." He slowly shook his head. "It's quite a tale, really."

"What is it?" Ellen asked nervously, leaning forward slightly.

Peter opened his book, to a spot he'd marked with a scrap of paper. "This is my great-grandfather's journal," he explained. "He fancied himself a historian, and hoped one day to have a history of Deepwater as it happened, so that others could look back and see how much it grew. He's a good number of these books, actually."

"What a wonderful idea he had," Ellen's mother said. "Have you considered copying them? Letting the café add them to the library?"

"You know, Alyssa said the same," Peter told her thoughtfully. "Maybe I will. Indeed, there's a good bit that's interesting in them. He's got more than a dozen. That's why it took me so long to find what you were asking about," he said to Ellen apologetically.

"You're here now, and that's all that matters," Ellen said. She shyly added, as she looked at her parents, "I'd asked Peter if he knew why our families didn't get along. He had hoped perhaps that was in one of the old journals."

"And it's right here," Peter said. "I'm going to paraphrase it. You see, many, many years ago, Al Clayton fell in love with a woman named Hilda. My great-grandfather described Hilda as a ray of sunshine. He spoke of how everyone liked her, male and female alike. She was always sweet-natured, clever, and not the least bit fussy. I'd found a story of a time she'd been knocked into our stream, and came out all muddy. She simply laughed about it."

"A much different response than I'd have had," Mrs. Clayton laughed, as Ellen and her mother nodded in agreement.

"Well, it all started when Gregory Grayson found himself paired with Hilda at a dance. He fell head over heels for her. A few days later, he planned to ask permission from her parents to court her. However, he hadn't realized that his best friend, Al Clayton, was also in love with Hilda, and had the same idea."

"So that's how it started," Derek whispered as he squeezed Ellen's hand.

"What happened next?" Reverend Sullivan asked, almost on the edge of his chair. A quick glance showed Ellen that everyone was riveted, focused entirely on Peter.

"As soon as Al and Gregory got to talking, they decided one thing," Peter continued.

"That was it? They broke off the friendship because of a woman," Ellen's father said. "Al must have gone behind Gregory's back, asked her anyway."

"You are quick to assume it wasn't the other way around," Mr. Clayton said, crossing his arms. "Be just like a Grayson to be the double-crosser."

"That's where you'd both be wrong," Peter said, quickly stopping the argument. "When they met, they decided the only thing to do, for the sake of their friendship, was to choose someone else to marry. As my great-grandfather wrote, 'Al said there were plenty of women on earth, but there was only one friendship as great as theirs. Gregory agreed, and by a miracle it seems, a wagon train that had a half dozen unmarried women broke down at Deepwater, and the two each married a woman from there.'"

There was silence as everyone took in the words. Ellen felt goosebumps rising on her arms. "Only one friendship as great as theirs," she whispered. "They proved that too, didn't they?"

Her father was looking a little sheepish as he glanced at Mr. Clayton. "Well, how'd the feud start then?"

"That's where the story gets even more interesting," Peter said. "Seem's Hilda was a bit of a runaround. She took what she could and hoped to have a long string of men to provide for her in comfort, and her plan was to lead them along but never commit. So, it was a good thing neither man married her. However, she did marry someone eventually, a fellow named Clark Buck. He didn't provide the way she'd hoped," Peter set down the book and then pulled another out of his jacket pocket, opening it, "and when they had children, she was so bitter, because by then both the Claytons and the Graysons were doing quite well for themselves, she and her children set to spreading all kinds of lies about one to the other."

"But surely, as good of friends as they were, they'd have gone to the other, and asked if what the first was saying was true," Ellen objected.

"Maybe, maybe not," Gabriel interjected. "Sometimes when pride is wounded, or someone's embarrassed, they get quite defensive. They'd rather hurt the other to try and make themselves feel better than not."

"Buck," Ellen's mother was muttering. "Buck."

"I don't know anyone by that name," Gabriel said.

"There was a family here by that name when I was growing up," Peter said. "I don't know what happened to them. I can check my father's journals, though. He also was keeping the history of Deepwater, like his father, and his father before him, and I do."

"Buck," Ellen's mother said again, and then she looked at Mrs. Clayton. "Lizzie Buck?"

Mrs. Clayton stiffened. "I remember her. Always trying to turn people against each other."

"I remember her too," Mr. Clayton said. A strange expression came over his face, and he said, "Sadie, I reckon I owe you, and Marta, and Glen an apology then."

Ellen wondered if the shocked expression on her face looked anything like the one Derek wore. He squeezed her hand again, and Ellen ventured to ask, "Did she try to cause problems for you too, Mr. Clayton?"

"Sure did," he answered. "Day before we married, she told me Glen here and Marta had been making fun of us." His voice lowered. "Of course, our families hadn't liked each other for some time by then. I wonder if that's because of the Buck family, but I believed it. Thinking I could spare Sadie from getting hurt, even though I'd told her she and Marta could still be friends, I changed my mind."

Mr. Clayton drew in a deep breath. "Seems like our families could have reunited a generation ago, but for that woman."

"And our stubbornness," Ellen's father said. He hesitated, and said, "She came to me as well, and said something similar. Hinted that you'd married Sadie because you couldn't have Marta. And I...I thought I'd protect Marta from you."

Everyone sat silently.

Finally, Mr. Clayton said, "I'm sorry. For a lot of things."

"I am too," Ellen's father said, and stood up, offering his hand. "What do you say we start fresh? Letting our clever wives and children lead by example?"

"There's nothing that I'd like better," Mr. Clayton said.

Ellen's eyes felt moist, and she didn't care if she cried. An incredible joy filled her. She watched with a watery smile as her mother and Derek's embraced, clinging to each other.

Derek whispered, "You did it," and Ellen looked into his eyes.

"Not me," she said with a smile. "We all did it. Each of us had some part in this reunion."

"Except for me," Gabriel sighed. "All I did was ask questions."

"And show up at the right time," Ellen laughed. "Your timing was impeccable."

"That wasn't me," Gabriel said, raising a hand and pointing upward. "I'd not planned to stop by, but I was on the wagon and here quite before I realized it."

"Good timing is God's timing," Mrs. Clayton said.

With nods, everyone took their seats again, and Ellen asked, softly, "May I ask, what happens next? Does this mean that Derek and I might be allowed to..."

She stopped. Might be allowed to what? Be friends? While that wasn't enough for her, was it what their parents might accept? She wasn't sure if she was even going to be able to be that. She was to be married after all.

Her head lowered. "Never mind. I just remembered I'm to be married tomorrow and sent away."

"Oh, Glen! Do something," her mother pleaded.

"I've got a wagon hitched and ready," the reverend offered, rising. "Where should we go?"

"I'll join you," Mr. Clayton said. "That is, if you'd be willing to accept my son courting your lovely daughter."

Ellen's eyes were wide, and she held her breath. Beside her, Derek was tense, and a combination of fear and worry played over his face. "Pa?" she whispered, standing up and pressing her hands into her stomach.

"Marta, I'll be back as soon as I can," he said, kissing his wife before heading to the wagon. "Got to call things off. William Stafford can find another bride. There's only one friendship like ours, and it's time we repaired it. We've already wasted enough time."

"I couldn't agree more. We'll stop by and get Hugh, let him know everything's going to be okay, and I think you ladies have some catching up to do," Mr. Clayton said with a wink, as he followed Gabriel and her father to the wagon.

"And, perhaps a wedding to plan," Mrs. Clayton said, coming over to Ellen, and hesitantly resting a hand on her arm.

"I do have a new fabric," Ellen whispered, her cheeks coloring. "It's a lovely green."

"I know just the one you got," Mrs. Clayton said. To Ellen's surprise, Derek's mother looked at him with a soft smile and added, "And I can't think of anyone more lovely to wear it."

Chapter 22

Derek could hardly believe the last few weeks. After Ellen's father had told the other man the wedding was off, he and Ellen had been allowed to court, just like any other couple in Deepwater.

There had been a church picnic, where the men bid on the ladies' baskets, and Derek had been pleased to win Ellen's, for the price of four dollars. She'd made some of his favorite foods, savory hand pies, garden pickles, apples, two types of cheese, potato salad, and mint tea. The desserts were potluck, and he'd further helped himself to a molasses pie by Carissa, and a blackberry pie by Mrs. Grayson.

Afterward, he and Ellen had taken a long walk back to her house, with him feeling mighty nervous the whole time. He'd already asked her father for permission to marry her, and he'd said yes. He even already knew that it was unlikely Ellen would say no. But when the moment came to ask her, he'd been a nervous wreck.

Derek chuckled to himself as he recalled how he'd stammered so much, Ellen hadn't been able to understand a word he'd said. He didn't know how many tries it had taken before he managed to spit the words out. "Ellen, will you marry me?"

Of course, she'd said yes, and wedding planning began in earnest. With help from his father and Ellen's, along with Hugh, Derek had built a small house for him and Ellen. It was on Clayton land, but not too far from where her parents lived.

And, after today, they'd be living there.

"You look nervous," Hugh said, thumping him on the back as he came up.

Derek laughed as he shook his head. "Sure am." He sobered then, as he looked up at his older brother. "I'm just sorry this wasn't done sooner, so you could have gotten the woman you wanted."

"I'll find one soon enough," his brother said confidently, then winked. "And if not, that's okay," Hugh said. "I'll find her eventually. Today, however, is about you. Ready to go in?"

Derek nodded. Today would be his last Sunday service as an unmarried man. As soon as church was over, the reverend would call him and Ellen forward to marry them.

He sucked in a breath full of nerves and excitement, and followed his brother inside, to their usual pew.

As everyone filed in, Dirk played soft music on the piano. Once everyone was seated, Gabriel addressed them.

"Dear friends, I'm so glad you are here today. I have a wedding to perform, so I will invite you all to stay after the service." His eyes sought Derek and then moved away, presumably to locate Ellen.

As Gabriel spoke of pride and redemption, Derek found himself glancing at his parents. Over the last few weeks, it felt like his mother was always with Ellen's. It seemed no time had passed for the two women, who had picked up right where they'd left off, ignoring the years of discontent.

Their fathers also had made an effort to get along. It would be slower going on that front, but Derek hoped it would happen.

When the service ended, Gabriel held up his hands. "And now, if you'd like to stay, I'm proud to be the one to join Derek Clayton and Ellen Grayson in marriage."

There was a buzzing of excited voices, and a few soft claps—they were in church after all. Derek rose and saw Ellen had done the same. They moved to the front of the church where they stood there, Ellen looking as nervous as Derek felt.

"Are you ready?" the reverend asked.

Ellen nodded the same time Derek did. Gabriel opened a small book, and read, "Dearly beloved, we are gathered together here in the sight of God, and in the face of this congregation, to join together..."

Derek's nerves rose again, until he looked into Ellen's eyes. Once they met, any tension or worries he'd had since the day he met her fled. Everything felt right. Perfect. He had no doubt in his mind that she felt the same, by the radiant smile she was giving him.

Gabriel continued, and then said, "If anyone present knows of any reason why these two should not be united in marriage, let them speak now or forever hold their peace."

Derek grinned at Ellen. Who would speak out? For once, he was entirely confident that nothing would interrupt this moment.

But just then, a man stood up from the back of the church, and yelled, "I do! I object!"

All around them, there were gasps filling the church. Ellen stepped closer to Derek, bewilderment on her face. "Who is that?" Derek asked.

"I've never seen him before," Ellen said.

Gabriel frowned, and stepped closer. "I don't know you, friend," he said. "Who might you be?"

"William Buck Stafford," the stranger said. "And she was to marry me!"

But one word had stood out, and caused not only Derek and Ellen and Gabriel to stiffen, but their parents to rise.

"Buck?" Derek's father said. "Did you say Buck?"

William smirked. "I did. Got a problem with it?"

"Sure do," Ellen's father said, stepping closer. "The Bucks have caused enough trouble. Now, you get going. I told you the wedding was off, and I meant it."

William started to smirk again, but then he saw that all around the church, the men and a good number of the women stood up in solidarity with the Graysons and Claytons. It warmed his heart, and Derek suspected it did the same to Ellen's.

A moment later, the church door closed, the man having left in haste, but Hank stood by a window, watching just the same.

"Well, then. How about we continue?" Gabriel asked.

"I'd like nothing more," Derek said, grinning down at Ellen who smiled shyly at him.

Before he'd realized it, Gabriel was saying, "You may kiss the bride."

Derek gave Ellen a gentle kiss, and then pulled back slightly, whispering, "I love you, Ellen."

He could hardly hear her echoing answer because Gabriel called out, "I now pronounce you, man and wife."

They took hands and walked down the center of the church together, and out into the sunshine. Within moments, they were surrounded by wellwishers. And, thankfully, no William Buck Stafford in sight.

His mother and Ellen's set to work along with several of the other women to set out the food they'd been working on for days. It was just a simple wedding meal, cold ham, biscuits, baked beans, and cookies, but everyone enjoyed it heartily.

As he looked around, Derek's eyes landed on Hugh, who was talking with a woman around his age. They were laughing about something, and Hugh looked happy, something he hadn't seemed for a long time. Derek couldn't help but hope whoever she was, she was the right person for him. Hugh deserved nothing less.

Derek sat with Ellen, one hand holding hers, as they rested in the spot they'd snuck to often, the large tree with the bench in the church's garden.

"Did you ever think we'd get to this point?" Ellen asked.

"I didn't," Derek answered her truthfully. "Because I thought nothing would bring our families together. I'm glad I was wrong."

"Such a Clayton," Ellen teased, "admitting his mistakes and then moving forward."

"And just like a Grayson," he answered, teasing in return, "Always so forgiving."

They laughed together, and Derek realized that nothing could be more perfect. But he was sure willing to spend the rest of his life seeing what came next. If he and Ellen had rebuilt their families' relationships after their forbidden romance, what more could they accomplish?

Great things. He was sure of that.

Epilogue

"A new generation," Ellen's mother whispered, as she stared down into the face of her new grandson. "And one who will move forward, never knowing the hatred we'd had for each other."

"It's all in the past now," Derek's mother agreed, as she finished wrapping the new baby's twin brother in a knitted blanket.

"Can we show them now?" Ellen asked excitedly, sitting up slightly in the bed.

"Yes, let them in," the midwife said, and stepped back.

As soon as Ellen's mother opened the door, Derek, followed by their fathers, rushed in. And then froze.

"Twins?" Derek gulped as he stared between his mother and Ellen's.

"That's right," Ellen said. "Can you think of anything better? And, I was thinking, perhaps we'd name them after their grandfathers. Just a little reminder, if we ever were to forget, about how linked our families are and how there's a new, beautiful, unsullied future ahead of them. What do you think?"

"I think we'll never need that reminder," Derek's father said, coming close and touching one of the baby's tiny fingers. "But I can't say I don't like the name." He grinned. "I'd be right proud to have a namesake."

"So would I," Ellen's father said.

"Welcome to the family, Little Joe and Glen," Ellen whispered to each of her sons. "You are loved more than you know." She looked up then, at her parents and Derek's, and said, "And so are you. I couldn't ask for a better family."

Derek smiled down at her, standing between their two fathers, and Ellen felt happiness wash over her, just before her eyes started to droop.

She was aware of their parents tiptoeing out, leaving the babies safe in the cradle Derek had labored over the last few months. Luckily, it was extra wide. Tiredly, she reached to her throat, where the heart Derek had made her rested on a chain he'd bought her, and closed her eyes.

"I'll stay," Derek whispered to her. "You sleep. Everything's fine now."

And it was. So much so, that it felt as though their families had always been together and united. Ellen let her head fall against the pillow and sleep wash over her.

There was no need to worry this happiness was a dream. She had Derek's love, and he had hers, forever.

What more stories from the town of Deepwater?

Watch for a new series, Hearts of Deepwater, starting in 2026. Until then, you might enjoy these other books, set in the town of Deepwater. Each is available in eBook, paperback, and large print.

***

Trapped in Deepwater (Gabriel and Laura's story)
https://www.amazon.com/Trapped-Deepwater-Christm as-Bride-Dilemma-ebook/dp/B0C74R6NW6
Alyssa's Desperate Plan (Alyssa and Peter's story)

https://www.amazon.com/Alyssas-Desperate-Rejected-Mail-Order-Brides-ebook/dp/B0CN8FKZX7

Mail-Order Tailor (Josiah and Ginny's story)

https://www.amazon.com/Mail-Order-Tailor-Husbands-Sarah-Lamb-ebook/dp/B0DR696PT4

Away in Deepwater (Samantha and Dirk's story)

https://www.amazon.com/Away-Deepwater-Christmas-Sweethearts-Historical-ebook/dp/B0DM6SPJDJ

Cherry Cheese Pie by Carissa (Carissa and Duncan's story)

https://www.amazon.com/Cherry-Cheese-Pie-Carissa-Holiday-ebook/dp/B0DDQJYMPT

Note from Author

Thank you for taking the time to read *Waiting in the Shadows*.

Could I ask for one small favor? Reviews like yours on Amazon mean so much to me and help others to find my books! Even just a single line means a lot!

Also...

Want a FREE book?

Stop by my website to get your no strings attached **FREE book**. It's my gift to you, as a thank you for reading this one.

www.sarahlambbooks.com

About the Author

Sarah writes captivating characters and clean romance that's anything BUT boring! From heartbreaking moments to heartwarming tales, get swept away in either historical or small town romance that pulls you in until the last page.

Nestled in the Blue Ridge Mountains of Virginia where she's married to her Texan husband, you'll find Sarah creating her next book, spending time with her children, or volunteering in her community.

Want more of Sarah's books? Find them all on Amazon!

https://www.amazon.com/stores/Sarah-Lamb/auth
or/B098H3SGLK